I0451955

WHEN IMAGINATIONS SPARK

STORIES ARE BORN

Scribes Valley Publishing
Knoxville, Tennessee
scribesvalley.com

ISBN: 978-1-7349744-6-1

Scribes Valley Publishing Company
Knoxville, Tennessee
www.scribesvalley.com

DEDICATION

This anthology is dedicated
to those who appreciate that special spark.

TO THE AUTHORS FEATURED IN THIS BOOK:

Scribes Valley Publishing sincerely thanks you
for your time, patience, trust, and talent.

TABLE OF CONTENTS

A STORY IS BORN
A Foreword by David L. Repsher, editor

A brain at rest, random thoughts flickering through its hinterlands, nothing registering, nothing sticking.

Then FLASH!

A tiny spark in the darkness that begins to burn, growing with every nanosecond, swelling ever larger, impossible to ignore, impossible to push away. It pulls in on itself, condensing, forming, solidifying...

A story in its infancy, trying to gather what it needs to survive. Drawing sustenance from the Imagination of the Author. Trying to mature. Trying to become a complete entity. Seeking the light of day, to make its way into the human world.

Finding and delighting other imaginations is the goal. To make tingle the fancy of others. To pull minds out of the here and now and send them down the many paths of Elsewhere.

Open your mind and allow the stories in this anthology to grab your imagination. Receive the sparks that started them. Receive the thrills, excitement, wonder, and triumph of them.

Become one with each of them.

Or, just read them one by one and marvel at their power. It's your choice.

FIRST PLACE

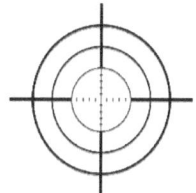

POP GOES THE WEASEL
©2025 by Dennis McFadden

Southwark, London, nightfall, October 7, 1971

Eoghan Grant had a gift, if quirks of olfaction could be considered as such. Often, and at the most unpredictable times, on the aroma of frying rashers, or on the dank air of a public house, he could make out the sickly-sweet scent of the flowers on his father's grave. Somehow that skill evolved within him over the years till one winter night on patrol near the border of County Armagh, he realized, miraculously, that if there were any within a mile of him, he could detect the cold iron smell of English guns. As there was no other explanation, Eoghan took it to be a gift straight from God.

Out of nowhere he could smell them. This night, less than a fortnight after they'd arrived at the Southwark safe house. He looked at the dusty clock on the parlor wall, beside the framed and faded old print of cows in an idyllic pasture. Half-six: time was up.

Hugh McGlynn was at the window. A frail lad with skin stretched taut, his hair shone out from his head like a wild, red halo. He was staring wistfully out through the fog in the street, hanging thick as wool on a spring lamb. The lad was homesick, Eoghan knew; sure, weren't they all, he supposed, but only on Hugh did it show.

"Jesus," said Hugh in his soft Cork drawl, "would you ever believe Mrs. Mumford out for a stroll on a night such as this? She'll

9

be after catching her death." Mrs. Mumford, an old lady with a cane and a wig, lived in the terrace house next door.

"Come away from the window, Hugh," said Eoghan, and his voice made them look up, Hugh from the window, Neil Crossnan and Brawler Daigle from the game, Crazy Eights, they were playing at the card table across the room. "Come away from the window. Fetch the masks."

"The masks?" Hugh said.

"They're here."

"Who's here?"

"Come away from the window."

Hugh frowned and gave his thatch of hair a scratch, as Brawler Daigle, all twenty stone of him, scarred ham cheeks tight in a grimace, made at once for the makeshift arsenal in the closet at the bottom of the stairway, Neil close behind. Still Hugh hesitated.

From out of the fog the faint muted clicking of boots on cobblestones.

Hugh was off to fetch the masks from the kitchen cupboard. Neil and Eoghan maneuvered the dusty piano with the cracked veneer that hadn't been played in decades across the front door off the parlor, while Hugh and Brawler shoved the oak sideboard in the kitchen across the back door. It was a terraced house, of brick construction: two front windows in the parlor facing the street, along with the front door, and two windows and a door facing the back garden from the kitchen; a lot for four men to defend. On either side was another terrace home, both of which by now were well and truly vacated, Eoghan suspected.

Eoghan went to the pantry. Under a cloth in a wooden box, like white dough rising, lay seven five-pound wedges of gelignite. Eoghan turned each tenderly. *Such a waste.* They'd had such grand plans for the stuff. *Such a waste.*

Fucking Mrs. Mumford, he thought. *What did Hugh tell her? Or was it his accent alone?*

Back in the parlor, Eoghan doused the lamp. The room was ghostly in the dim light, the familiar furnishings darkened, eerie, uncertain. Three men standing in the gloaming, faces bright, eyes searching, frozen in the moment on the cusp of eternity.

Hugh said, "You're after turning the jelly?"

"I am," Eoghan said.

"Why bother," said Hugh, "if they're here? What's the difference now?"

"Professional standards," said Eoghan, "I'd rather not go out like a bloody amateur."

"*Pop goes the weasel*," sang Neil Crossan, his wide face made wider by his black beard, his Belfast smirk nearly visible in the half-light. Brawler Daigle looked over, a child's wonder on his face at the sudden sound of a child's verse—Brawler might have been the strongest man in the army, but certainly not the brightest—while Eoghan smiled a wary smile, a close eye on Neil, *Crazy Eights Crossnan*, fucking crazy Neil.

When Neil was answered by another series of clicks from outside, he began to sing even louder, standing to tap his foot in time to the tune, breaking into a bit of a jig, using his rifle as a stage-prop cane, smiling all his teeth, singing,

"All around the mulberry bush,
The monkey chased the weasel.
The monkey stopped to pull up his sock,
Pop! goes the weasel."

Eoghan didn't know whether to laugh or cry or tell Neil to shut the hell up. He knew the reasons for the shenanigans, of course, besides Neil being a lunatic and being scared to death, as were they all; he didn't want Hugh to hear the fresh clicking sounds. Of them all, Hugh was the only one who'd never heard the sound of an SLR magazine being rammed home for action.

Eoghan appreciated the irony, he'd always had a fine appreciation of the stuff, thinking about all the rebel songs depicting all the noble ends of Irish martyrs, Kevin Barry, Roddy McCorley, Sean South, and here were the four of them, marching to glory to the tune of "Pop Goes the Weasel."

He said, "Neil, would you ever get the fuck down."

The phone rang, a blast that shot through the room like a power surge.

Hugh yelped.

"Easy there, little fella, easy," Brawler Daigle said.

Neil said, "Sure, Hugh, they're only calling for an encore."

They all had a soft spot for Hugh, for the youngest, for the virgin. He was far too young, but he was also far too valuable not to be there. He'd taught himself a trade, having mastered it by the time he was seventeen, when he'd joined the army to ply it. Hugh McGlynn knew more about explosives than any other man in the brigade; the stuff was second nature to him, instinctive as the handling of a football or hurley is to some men. He could shape a charge with such skill and precision it could blow a hundred yards. He'd swapped his boyhood for the skill, for that and its medium, the wild-eyed, romantic Republicanism about which he'd read and dreamed since he was a wee lad in Cork, in rebel County Cork.

Hugh had joined the struggle out of love. The others had joined out of hate.

Eoghan picked up the phone.

"Owen Grant?" The voice on the other end, a crisp, upper-class British accent.

"Sherlock Holmes?" said Eoghan.

"Elementary, my dear Owen—it had to be yourself or Neil Crossnan. Daigle's too stupid to know which end of the phone to speak into, and poor Hugh McGlynn, his big-boy pants must be quite soiled by now."

"Well, forgive me, Mrs. Mumford." Eoghan shook his head, heart sinking. It was not Mrs. Mumford who'd given them away. She didn't know Neil, didn't know Brawler or him. There was a grass, a supergrass, somewhere in the upper echelons of the army command. Eoghan had suspected—feared—as much.

"Shall we forget Mrs. Mumford for the time being? I'm sure you've more urgent matters on your mind at the moment."

"What are you offering?"

"What am I offering? What do you suppose I'm offering? Your

lives. You come out now, peacefully, and you don't die. Simple as that."

"Classic in its simplicity."

"We're not prepared for a siege. It ends now. You come out, under your own power, or a bit later, in tidy bags."

Eoghan stopped, set his jaw. Six eyes staring at him through the gloom.

He said, "Let me see what the lads have to say."

"Do you want my opinion, Owen?"

Eoghan said nothing.

"It's foolish to fight. Foolish to die. You've no war in the first place, and even if you did, it's properly over now. You haven't a prayer of survival, which I expect you know. And consider this, Owen. The days for the making of Irish martyrs are over. There'll be no more Clanabogans. You won't gain a thing by your dying. If we have to kill you, I promise we'll blow up the place and announce to the world it was your own bloody fault—trying to put together a bomb to kill innocent civilians, you mishandled the jelly. And there wasn't a Tommy on this side of the Thames."

"They won't believe it."

"They will, Owen. They've always believed it. They always will."

"Give me some time to talk to the lads."

"Five minutes. Not a tick more."

Eoghan pressed the phone slowly back into its cradle as if to smother it and looked at the men in the room. Six eyes staring back at him through the gloom, three grim faces. "Well, boyos?" he said.

"Whatever you say, Eoghan," said Neil.

"Sure," said Brawler, "you're the one giving the orders."

"What did they say on the phone?" said Hugh.

"What difference does it make?" Brawler said. "We follow orders, little fella."

"We're all baking in the same oven," Eoghan said. "I won't be after ordering any man to stay without hearing what he has to say first."

"I say we stay," said Neil.

"If we're voting," said Brawler, "I say we stay and kill some of the bastards."

"Of course you do, Brawler," Eoghan said. "Now here's what he told me—if we surrender, walk out now, we can live. That's all. No promises, no guarantees, no discussion, nothing else. If we fight, they'll kill us all and blow the place up and announce to the press we accidently set off our own bomb—like bloody amateurs. They won't have the lads making martyrs out of us."

"How'll they explain the fire fight?" said Neil.

"They've cleared the area. They'll dispense the statements. Classic cover-up."

"Sure, we could hold out for hours," Brawler said, convincing himself. "Hours."

Eoghan didn't like the wildness of the glint beginning to show in his eyes.

"I'm only thinking if we surrender," Hugh said, "we might live to fight another day."

"I suppose, Hugh," Eoghan said. "There's always that hope."

"Shit," said Neil.

"You'd have to survive the torture first," Brawler said.

"Torture?" said Hugh.

"*Interrogation*," Neil said.

"Sure," said Hugh, "we could survive a few beatings. Couldn't we?"

"The beatings are only the beginning," Brawler said.

"The beatings are between the torture," mumbled Neil.

"*Enough*," Eoghan said. Then, to Hugh, "I'm afraid there is a bit more to it, Hugh."

"That's the way the money goes," Neil said, "pop! goes the weasel."

Hugh, his sweaty face growing paler in the shadows, said, "Listen—if they know about us, then maybe they know the rest. Maybe they've no need of interrogating at all."

"That's not the way it works, little fella," Brawler said.

"It doesn't matter what we know," Neil said. "It's what we done."

"It's what we are," Eoghan said.

"So, Neil and me, we vote stay," said Brawler. "Eoghan, what's your vote?"

Eoghan only looked at Hugh, a soft, resigned expression they'd seldom seen.

"It's *madness* to stay," said Hugh. Then, with less conviction, "Isn't it?"

Neil reached for the deck of cards on the nearby table. "Pick a card," he said, "any card."

Brawler climbed to his feet. The eyes of him were glazed and slippery.

"Brawler!" Eoghan said. "Brawler—stay at your post."

But Brawler made for Hugh, lumbering across creaking floorboards, his big, strong heart swamped. "Brawler," Eoghan said, "stay the hell down!" But Brawler paid no heed. The big man knelt beside Hugh, took him gently by the shoulders. "It'll be all right," he said in a rumbling coo. "It'll soon be over. Just be brave. Just be brave for a little while. Pearse and Connolly are waiting for us up there."

"Ah Jesus," Neil said. "Are you going to burp him too?"

"They are waiting for us," Brawler said. "All the brave Irishmen!"

"Brawler," said Eoghan, "stay the hell down! Get back to your post!"

The big man whirled away from Hugh. Glinting through the gloom were the tears on his fat, scarred cheeks. A huge snuffling and his big arm came across his face.

"Brawler?" said Eoghan. "Brawler? Are you wanting to change your vote?"

"Jesus, no. What, you think I'm going yellow?"

"No—nobody's saying any such thing."

"I'm not, Eoghan. I'm not," His hand reached over to touch Hugh's knee with a gentle squeeze. "It's just that...I want to fight them...But Jesus...I am scared, you know. I'm scared of one thing, by Jesus—I'm scared if one of them fuckers kills me before I have a chance to kill some of them first. Please God, please, don't let me die without killing at least one of those murdering British fuckers first, God, please."

"Dear God," Neil said, glancing heavenward. "I'll wager you don't get that sort of a prayer every day. Amen."

The telephone rang.

Brawler snuffled again. "Let me, Eoghan!"

"Stay put," Eoghan said. "Get back to your post."

He never considered the contradiction in his order as the phone rang again, and Brawler stood, stomping toward the phone, floorboards shivering, Eoghan warning again, "Stay *down*!"

Brawler snatched up the phone.

"*Down!*" Eoghan said, a last time, but the big man didn't hear, nor did he hear the blast out of the fog, the bullet piercing the glass and his head, an eruption of red in the twilight spraying out behind him. Knocked backward two baggy steps, he was still for an instant, remains of his face frozen in surprise, toppling like a giant oak.

"Christ," whimpered Hugh, "Mother of God."

Neil smiled broadly through his beard, turned back to his window. "Pop goes the weasel," he said, smashing the window with the butt of his rifle, opening fire.

Eoghan fired his Thompson, harsh, clipped bursts into the fog, one after another, and a tidal wave of noise descended, a vibrating thunder, as the waves of return fire commenced, a hundred competing explosions, hammering bricks, shattering wood and glass and everything else in the universe, wild ricochets whining, the fiery clangor of bullets bursting on stone and brick. With the first volley came the canisters of CS gas, filling the flat with acrid fumes as thick as the fog outside, even before the fog itself tumbled in through the splintered windows. Eoghan was pinned, firing over his head, seeing nothing, the fire was too intense and sustained. Hearing Neil maintaining a steady return fire from the back, he realized none was coming from Hugh's position. "Shoot your gun, man, fire back!" though he doubted the boy could hear the order. He heard something then he thought he imagined, something different from Neil's position, ghostly, incongruous, barely discernible, but real, the dry quavering voice of Neil Crossnan, grotesquely muffled by his mask,

"Half a pound of tuppenny rice,
Half a pound of treacle.
Mix it up and make it nice,
Pop! goes the weasel."

On came the fusillade, ebbing, flowing, yet ever intense, salvo after salvo. Eoghan in a dazed wonder at the sheer, overwhelming force of the firepower. He couldn't aim a shot, it was that heavy, only managing quick, useless bursts above his head before flattening. The sweat had dried on his skin like a brittle shell, his heart beating out through it all as if to shatter the shell. He found himself alone.

Isolated at the heart of the cacophony, wrapped in the cloud of fog and fumes like a shroud, wincing at the jagged edges, muffled by his mask. Numbed utterly by dread and noise. *Pop! goes the weasel.* His da came to his mind, first the grave, the smell of the flowers, then the man, big man, twice the size of wee Eoghan, standing in the doorway out of the rain, his shirt in rags, his face rough and creased and flashing all those big white teeth in a smile for his boy. Eoghan realized with a start that this was his sinking, his life flashing before his eyes, and he brought himself back from the brink.

The return fire began to slacken oh so slightly, growing monotonous and ordinary, and he slowly became aware that he alone was firing from the flat.

"Neil? Neil! Hugh!"

No answer. The fumes had risen, thinning to ghostly wisps at floor level. He crawled toward Neil's window.

...up and down the city street...,

Neil Crossnan was dead. Face down on his rifle, his life's blood fleeing across the floor, away from him. Eoghan crawled away, through the blood.

...in and out the Eagle...

He found Hugh in from the wall, behind the davenport, near the body of Brawler Daigle. He was shivering, chilled with sweat.

Eoghan shook him by the shoulders. "Hugh! Hugh, lad! Come out of it!"

The eyes of Hugh were blank, unseeing.

"Hugh! Have ye fired your weapon?"

He gave a small, tentative, negative nod. He shuddered, wracked by a new assault of shivering. Eoghan removed his mask, then Hugh's, sweat pouring out of each, then reached for the needlepoint throw on the davenport, and wrapped it around the skinny shoulders. Hugh clutched at the thing. The gunfire from beyond eased up.

Eoghan smiled. "You look like an oul woman."

The smile on the face of Hugh appeared and fluttered away again just as quickly, the work of a sorcerer. His lips clenched and loosened. "Jesus, Eoghan, I can't do it."

"Can't do what, lad? Can't shoot your gun?"

"No. Not that." The gunfire had nearly ceased altogether. Hugh's voice had gone to a calm sing-song, a lullaby; he was back in his native Cork. "No, I can't stand up, Eoghan. In front of the window. I wanted to stand up in front of the window, but I hadn't the courage to."

"That's not a way to go, Hugh."

"Doesn't matter, does it? What way we go?"

"It matters. It matters to your mortal soul."

Hugh's skinny ribs heaved a great sigh. "Do I even have a soul anymore? Or did I sell it? Did the devil take it?"

Eoghan snatched his jersey front with a rough fist, pulled the pale blinking face close to his. "I'll not listen to such talk. All the soulless bastards are on the *other* side of these walls, Hugh, on the other side, out there. You, you're a proud member of *Oglaigh Na hEireann*, the Army of the Republic of Ireland, and you gave up your boyhood, you gave up your very life, to right eight hundred years of wrong. You devoted yourself to the most just of causes— soul to the devil be damned."

The panic came to Hugh's face, again, the eyes darting wildly, beads of sweat across the fair forehead. "What am I to do, Eoghan?

What am I to do? I can't face their torture and I'm too scared to let them kill me—I'm too afraid for either. What am I to do?"

"Easy, laddie, easy." Hugh curled up in a ball at Eoghan's feet, whimpering, cursing, praying. Eoghan patted the back of his neck, wet and sticky with sweat. He didn't know how to answer the boy.

...round and round the mulberry bush...

He was right, Hugh was; he couldn't face the torture. Nor was it in the best interests of the army that he be allowed to do so. He was from the Free State, and that was the trouble; he had love enough of the republic, but not nearly enough hatred of the British. He hadn't lived it, hadn't seen every day firsthand the evil they could rise to. He couldn't hate them enough to withstand the pain. "You were a fine soldier, Hugh—you know that, don't you?"

The face looked up, pale and red, strained and wretched. "I was?"

"Ach, Jesus, are you codding me? One of the best, Hugh, one of the best. By God, you could shape a charge—I never saw such pretty blow-ye-ups in all my days."

"I was good at that—*that* I was good at."

"The best."

From close beyond the near window, Hugh's window, came the call of a voice. "Owen! Owen Grant! Are you in there? Is anybody?" The same voice from the phone.

Eoghan fired a quick burst from his Thompson toward the voice and another fusillade ensued, another broadside. Eoghan and Hugh shrank behind the davenport, a bullet ripping through the thing an inch from Hugh's ear, with a sharp whine and a seared, singeing scent, and Hugh cringed and whimpered and tried to shrink himself up into an even smaller ball.

Pity, thought Eoghan, the nearness of the bullet—pity it was not quite near enough.

...the monkey thought it was all in fun...

And then his da was there again, the smell of the flowers on his grave carried on the singed scent of the stuffing ripped out of the davenport. Again, the fire ebbed, slowing, slowing, easing into morbid stillness. Hugh remained in his ball, a fetal position, his breathing made up of billowing whimpers, his trousers soiled, the odors lifting up, trying to obliterate the smell of the flowers. Eoghan pictured the big hands of his da holding the scattergun, out by the shanty in the twilight of a spring evening, guiding the scattergun, nudging it close behind the ear of Angela, the old cow who'd broke her leg in a bog hole. Old Angela, whimpering, writhing in agony.

Eoghan set aside his Thompson, took his revolver from his belt behind his back. He patted the round, humped back of Hugh, who never looked up, feeling the totem pole of his spine, feeling the wracked breathing, the pain shooting though him in surges.

...pop! goes the weasel...

About the author:

Dennis McFadden, a retired project manager, lives and writes in a cedar-shingled cottage called Summerhill in the woods of upstate New York. His first collection "Hart's Grove," was published by *Colgate University Press* in 2010, and his second, "Jimtown Road," won the 2016 *Press 53* Award for Short Fiction; another collection, "Lafferty, Looking for Love," is forthcoming from *Cornerstone Press*. His novel, "Old Grimes Is Dead," earned a starred review from Kirkus Reviews, and was selected by their editors as one of the Best Indie Books of 2022.

Over a hundred of his stories have appeared in publications such as *The Missouri Review* (including the winner of the 2023 Perkoff Prize), *New England Review*, *The Sewanee Review*, *Arts & Letters*, *The Antioch Review*, *Ellery Queen Mystery Magazine*, *Alfred Hitchcock Mystery Magazine*, *The Best American Mystery Stories* and in the inaugural volume of the series, *The Best Mystery Stories the Year 2021*. A Pushcart Prize nominee, he also frequently serves as the judge for Prime Number Magazine's Short Fiction Award, and as their guest short fiction editor.

SECOND PLACE

SOMEWHERE SOUTH
©2025 by Terry Sanville

Dawson Melburn stood, grabbed his rucksack and tossed it onto the ground. He jumped down from the rear of the pickup and moved along its driver's side to the cab.

"Thanks, mister, for the lift. You sure this is the Blakely place?"

The old man behind the wheel gave him a toothy grin. "Oh yeah. Can't ya see? Them alfalfa fields are 'bout ready for mowin'...and Joy and Jacob will need help now that their sons are overseas."

"Yeah, that's what you said. I hope you're right."

"Well, if things don' work out with them, there're other farms along this road that might hire ya on."

"Thanks again."

With a *thunk*, the old man let off the brake and the pickup jerked forward, leaving a rooster tail of dust that hung thick in the afternoon heat. Dawson gazed across the wide-open fields toward the dark woods that snaked into the Sierra foothills, following the river. It looked green and tan to the horizon with town at least an hour behind him.

He'd spent the entire morning and part of the afternoon sitting on the porch of the feed store, asking local farmers if they needed help. They'd stare, like people used to at Wanted posters in the Post Office, check out his military-style haircut, three-day beard growth and tattered clothes, then brush past him. The old guy driving the pickup had been the exception.

"Local farmers need help; but you're not from 'round here and the bigger farms hire from contractors. Ya gotta find someone that'll trust you. Where's your folks, anyways?"

"I don't have much; my parents are gone, and I've got a brother somewhere in Texas."

"That's a big state."

"Yeah. Besides, he doesn't want to be found, by me or anybody."

"Huh. Family trouble never seems ta go away."

"That's the truth."

The sound of the pickup died, and the quiet afternoon settled in, broken by the *coo* of mourning doves. Hefting the rucksack onto his shoulder, Dawson headed down the long dirt track toward the two-story farmhouse, barns, and tractor sheds. Heat shimmered up above the fields, rich with the smell of alfalfa.

As he approached the house, he noticed the profile of a woman standing at an upstairs window: slender, old or young he couldn't tell, and dressed in some kind of robe. She turned to face the window and adjusted her gown, showing flashes of nakedness. In a moment, the window's curtains jerked shut.

At the house, he pushed through a rickety gate and set his rucksack down at the base of the porch steps. Before he could climb them, a woman right out of the *American Gothic* painting pushed through the screen door—definitely not the young lady he'd glimpsed through the upstairs window.

"If you're sellin' something, you can turn right around and vamoose," she said.

Daw smiled. "Well, I'm only selling myself. My name is Dawson Melburn and I'm looking for work. An old guy from town said you might need some help bringing in your alfalfa."

"I'll bet it was McGregor that told you that, such a nosey fella. You ever worked alfalfa?"

"No ma'am, but I can operate just about any machine with wheels or treads."

"Where you coming from?"

"I got a ride in from the Interstate this morning. Before that I've been around. Picked apples in Washington, dug early potatoes in Idaho."

"Wait here. I'll go get my husband. You know, we can't pay more than the minimum, but we can throw in meals and a place to stay during harvest."

"That works for me."

Dawson watched the woman hustle toward the barn. He lowered himself painfully onto the porch steps. The sun baked his body. But he also felt something else, something over his shoulder, standing behind the screen door, watching.

Before he could turn and look, the woman and a balding, bearded man emerged from the barn and moved toward him. The man might have been robust in his youth. But time and gravity had taken their due and the bent figure looked weary from decades of farm labor.

"My name's Jacob," he said and extended a hand.

"I'm Dawson. I was telling your wife that I'm looking for work."

"Well, jus' so happens that McGregor was right. I could use some help. Got two hundred acres of alfalfa to mow and take to the processor or the feedlots down valley."

Daw glanced sideways at the house. Something moved behind the screen, but he couldn't tell who or what. "Well, I can help with that."

"So...so you're not in trouble with the law or anything, are you?" Jacob asked. "We won't hire criminals to work here."

Daw grinned. "No, I'm a good person. I work hard. Keep to myself." He winced and rubbed the back of his left thigh.

"You got a hitch in your get-along?" Jacob asked.

"Just a piece of shrapnel I picked up in Afghanistan."

"So, you've served?"

"Yeah, three, actually two-and-a-half tours before they sent me home."

"Our sons are there now. They joined together...set to be

discharged next March. This is their second tour."

Daw studied the couple's faces. The woman's lips trembled, and the man stared at the ground. "I hope they stay safe. Things are winding down over there, and they all should be coming home soon."

"So, you've worked farms before?"

"For the last couple years, following harvests throughout the West."

"Is that all your gear?" Jacob pointed to the battered rucksack.

"Yes, that all I've got. Not much to show for twenty-seven years."

Jacob smiled and motioned Dawson inside. "Joy here will show you to your room. It's Frank's, my youngest son. We eat supper at six, and we'll talk more about work. It'll take three weeks to mow and bale this crop, maybe longer. My sons usually are here during harvest. The last couple of seasons have been tough."

"I learn fast. We can get at it tomorrow."

"Good, good," Jacob said, and moved off toward the barn.

Joy seemed to warm by a degree or two and took him through the front door to the back of the house and his room, instructed him on what closet to stow his things, what dresser drawers to use.

"I won't disturb anything of your son's," Daw said. "I'd kind of like to shower before supper."

"It's at the end of the hall. Hope you like simple country cooking."

"I'm sure it'll be great."

After showering, Daw lay on the bed and let the hot valley air finish the drying. He closed his eyes and found himself in a dusty Afghan city, its streets deserted.

The sound of rifle fire and exploding RPGs fills the air. Ahead, a man and a familiar-looking woman dash from a doorway and try crossing the street. The man stumbles and turns toward the advancing Americans, fear or hatred in his eyes, Daw can't tell which.

"Grenade!" someone shouts followed by the crack of weapons. The Afghani lays like a pile of dirty rags in the street. The woman

kneels beside him, wailing. The platoon pushes forward, not stopping, and moves into the heart of the city, taking fire and shouting out warnings all the way.

Someone shook his shoulder, and he opened his eyes.

"You were hollerin'," Joy said. She had spread a quilt over his half-naked body. "Bad dream I suppose. Do ya have them often?"

"Sorry, I don't want to disturb anyone. Maybe I should sleep in the barn."

"Nonsense. My sons write me, tell me they sometimes have the same thing, dreams that wake them at night."

"Yes, it's common."

"Better get dressed. Supper's in a little while."

As Dawson pulled on clean but terminally wrinkled clothes, the floorboards above him creaked. Somebody paced the upstairs room in bare feet. Daw hadn't asked about the mystery woman, figuring that he'd find out at supper. But neither Joy nor Jacob had volunteered anything. Had McGregor told him all he needed to know about that farm and the people who lived there? As he joined the couple in the kitchen, he noticed a fourth place-setting on the table.

"Are we expecting someone else?" he asked Joy as she dished out mashed potatoes, roast beef slices and something green.

Joy and Jacob looked at each other. "We thought that Grace would join us for dinner," Joy said, "but she said she'll grab somethin' later."

The silence between them grew until Daw asked, "So...so who is Grace?"

Jacob cleared his throat, "She's my oldest son's wife. She's staying with us until Erick comes home."

"That's...that's good of you to take her in."

Joy smiled. "They were rentin' a place in town when Erick enlisted. She's only got grandparents back east. It was easier for her to move in with us."

"That makes sense."

After supper, filled with chitchat about the farm and the work

Daw and Jacob would do the following days, they moved to the living room and watched bad network TV. The couple turned in at ten and Daw followed their example. He lay in the dark, listening to loud cricket sounds coming through his open window. Above him, all was silent except for a faint squeaking sound, like bedsprings being depressed.

He woke before dawn, before anyone else was up, or so he thought. Dressing in the darkness, he grabbed his cigarettes and moved stealthily down the hall and out the front door onto the porch. With the moon down, the stars shone extra bright. He stood at the railing and stared upward at meteors streaking across the sky.

"Beautiful, aren't they."

Daw clamped down hard on his urge to shout and turned to his right, toward the sound of the voice. "You...you startled me. You must be Grace."

"That's me, the prodigal wife. The Perseid meteor showers are just about over. You should have been here a couple of days ago."

"Yeah."

The silence built, the glow of her cigarette providing the only indication that she was there.

"So, you're the new hire. Where are you coming from?"

"Here and there. I've been on the move for the last couple of years."

"What's your name?"

"I'm sorry, I shoulda said. I'm Dawson Melburn. You can call me Daw."

"All right, Daw. So, what did Ma and Pa Kettle tell you about me?"

"Not much, except you're the wife of their eldest son."

"Yeah, Erick. That son of a bitch ditched me for a war zone."

"And you have grandparents back—"

"Yeah, that's what they tell everybody."

"So, it's not true?"

"Let's just say it's part of the mystery that is Grace."

"I like mysteries. I'm just terrible at solving them."

"Nobody's asking you to."

"Fair enough."

"So, you got a girl? Or do you swing the other way?"

Daw sighed. "Past tense. We broke up when I came back from overseas."

"So, she didn't like Daw 2.0?"

"Long story."

"Yeah, so's mine."

The silence settled in. Dawson stared at the sky and counted the falling stars, picturing the tiny meteors burning up in the atmosphere after being abandoned by a comet that takes more than a century to pass by again. He wondered if he would ever pass by his home again after what happened. When he glanced sideways, the denser darkness of Grace had slipped away into the night.

In the following days it was worse than reveille in the Army. Daw woke at five, ate a hearty breakfast, and readied himself for work at dawn. With few instructions from Jacob, he operated the self-propelled swather that cut the alfalfa. Jacob followed with the baler. The first few days they created large, rolled bales of green alfalfa. Another tractor attachment was used to grasp the bales and place them onto the bale wagon. From there Jacob disappeared along the farm road, towing the wagon to the processor three miles down.

"We'll leave some of the bales dry a bit before taking them to the feed lots," Jacob explained.

"No problem. But just tell me where to go and I can do it."

"Nah, that's my job. Besides, I like jawing with the folks at the processor, see how many of my neighbors are doing the same thing."

"What does the processor do?" Daw asked.

"They grind up the crop and compress it into pellets that are fed to livestock."

"Cool."

"Cool?"

Daw laughed. "Sorry, I'm still learning farm talk."

"So, you're a city boy?"

"Yeah, from the big smoggy."

"Huh, go figure."

While Jacob was away at the processor or the feedlots, Daw cleaned and serviced the machines and spent time in his room, reading. After the first few days he explored the woods that bordered the river, more like a large creek that fled the foothills. It was there that he finally met Grace in the daylight. He had caught glimpses of her passing between rooms. But she kept to herself and wouldn't share a meal with the rest of them.

The wind was blowing cold that late afternoon when he found her huddled on the ground watching the flowing creek. She had long red hair, fair skin and showed plenty of it in her loose housedress; a Virginia Slim dangled from full lips. Daw approached slowly, purposefully making sounds.

She whipped around. "What do you want?" she demanded, looking really pissed.

"I'm sorry to disturb you. I'll leave you alone." He turned to retreat.

"No...no, you don't have to. You just startled me, that's all."

"We don't have to speak. I can be quiet too."

"Sit your ass down and talk to me. I don't have much of a chance out here in the boondocks. And Joy is...well, she's not joyful."

"I understand. I take it you're not a farm girl."

"No shit, Sherlock."

"Neither am I...a girl...or from a farm."

Grace smiled. "Good to know."

Dawson went silent and stared at the creek, as if the right questions and answers might flow by and he could snatch them up and use them to talk with this beautiful woman. It had been years.

"So how long have you been living out here?" he asked.

"It's been almost a year since Erick was deployed. I've been here the whole time...well, most of it."

"Moving in with the in-laws, that must have been tough."

"Yeah, it was, but better than the alternative."

"The alternative?"

Grace turned toward Daw, and he stared into her green unblinking eyes. "Yeah, the alternative, the nut house."

"So that's part of your mystery?"

"Mystery is a nice way to put it. When I'm with Erick and take my meds, I'm a high-functioning schizophrenic. But when I'm not with him, with someone, I start to freak out and the people in my head take over. The shrinks felt it would be best that I live out here in the sticks rather than suffer the stress of the city."

"That makes sense, sort of."

"So now you know about me, warts and all."

Daw grinned. "No, we've hardly scratched the surface."

"But it's your turn, what do *your* warts look like?"

"Nothing spectacular or super ugly. I worked as a construction equipment mechanic out of Riverside. Joined the Army, for some stupid reason I still can't figure out. Spent too much time in Afghanistan. Came home to find some Jody screwing my fiancée. I've been traveling around ever since the...the breakup."

"Ah, another wounded warrior."

"Yeah, something like that."

"But you seem high functioning to me."

Dawson laughed. "Yeah, most of the time, sure, high functioning."

During the following days, Daw met Grace at the creek on afternoons when Jacob was off on deliveries and Daw finished with maintenance. She described her life to him: some stories rang true while others seemed made up; Daw couldn't always tell the difference. She'd stumble along, spouting strange lectures about human evolution, national politics, dying from some terrible disease, her thoughts and speech broken, scrambled. Other times she was the most articulate person Daw had ever met. And sometimes he'd find her huddled on the ground, arms wrapped around her knees, eyes squeezed shut and muttering to the voices in her head, unable to speak with Daw.

They didn't stay together long and always returned to the house separately. But Daw knew that Joy knew about their meetings, and she confronted him one evening on the front porch.

"I know you're seein' Grace down at the crick."

"Yes, we talk."

"So, you know she's sick."

"Yes."

Joy sighed. "She seems fine when she's with Erick. But alone out here, she can act real loony."

"I know."

"You be careful what you do with her. Erick loves that gal terribly. But she seems better after she's been with you. Just watch yourself, and don' do nothin' stupid."

"I hear you. I know what it's like..."

"I figured you might."

In the following days, Joy's words stuck in Daw's mind as he worked on maintaining the machinery in the tractor shed. The baler needed major work—an old model that would need a complete and expensive overhaul in the near future. He jumped when Grace laid a hand on his shoulder.

"Come with me," she said.

"Where we going?"

"Joy is working in her garden out by the west field and the place is empty."

Grace took his hand and led him back to the house, moving silently across the porch, through the screen and upstairs to her room.

"I don't let anyone else come in here. But I want you to."

She pulled him inside. All the window curtains were drawn back, and blinding light bathed the cluttered room, a space so chaotic that it looked like it had been touched by a tornado. Only a single clear path led from the door to the bed. She pulled him along and pushed him down onto the mattress.

"I want you," she whispered, and slipped out of her dress with nothing beneath.

Daw stared at her slender beauty, his heart thundering. She came into his arms, her body soft, smelling of the fields, of earth and pent-up passion. But he gently slipped her grip and sat up.

"What's wrong?" she asked. "Don't I turn you on?"

"Oh God, yes. I've been struggling to keep my hands off you these past weeks."

"Well, why the hell have you?"

"I just can't do it."

"You can't or you won't?" She stood before him, hands on hips, swaying.

"Won't."

"Why the hell not?"

"I...I won't be a Jody."

"What the fuck are you talking about?"

"Remember, I told you. When I came back from Afghanistan and found my fiancée sleeping with this other guy. I...I won't be that guy."

"Ah come on, nobody's gonna know. Erick's just a big lovable teddy bear. He's too dense to figure it out."

"Yeah...but *I* will know, and it'll drive me.... I know how it feels. I can't be that guy."

"How it feels? What about me?"

"Erick will come back to you soon. You just gotta hang on."

Dawson left before he could change his mind.

Less than a week later, Jacob pulled the last load of alfalfa bales to the feedlots down valley. Prices were good and Joy and Jacob's mood improved as the harvest neared its end. The following day, Jacob planned on driving Daw into town, to visit their bank and pay him his wages.

His last night on the farm, Dawson packed his rucksack, his clothes clean and ready for his next adventure. He had steered clear of Grace the last few days and hoped to slip away in the morning before she was up. Daw showered and went to bed early, not long after supper, while Joy and Jacob watched TV.

He woke when a car's headlights flashed across his wall. In a moment, car doors opened and closed and the front gate creaked. Stiff footsteps, as if driven by hardened souls, pounded on the porch, and then a knock on the front door.

Whoever it was, Joy invited them in and took them into the living room. Mumbled voices, silence, then more conversation too low to make out what was said. Silence. The minutes ticked by. The front screen opened then clicked shut. The car started. Daw forced himself out of bed and stared out the window at the tan sedan with government plates, like the ones Army officers used, moving slowly away.

He got back in bed and listened to what sounded like sobbing. Joy and Jacob climbed the stairs and knocked on Grace's door. In a moment it opened, more mumbled words, then nothing for a few minutes. Daw jumped when the door was slammed shut. The sound of things crashing against walls echoed throughout the house.

Daw lay awake and listened in the sad silence until he finally drifted off.

He woke with the sun up, past eight. Daw hurriedly dressed, grabbed his rucksack and hustled to breakfast. In the kitchen he found Jacob sitting at the table, nursing a cup of coffee.

"I've already et," he muttered. "Grab yourself some cornflakes then let's hit the road."

Daw nodded. In a few minutes they moved out the door and across the yard to the Dodge pickup parked next to the tractor shed. Daw climbed in and they drove off toward town. After a few miles he couldn't stay quiet.

"So, what's going on? I heard the ruckus last night. Is everything all right?"

"No...the...the Army chaplain came a callin'."

"Shit."

"Yeah, shit is right. They told us Erick was killed by an IED. My other boy, Frank, is bringing his body home and that...that..." Jacob let out a low sob and swiped at his eyes.

"I'm...I'm so sorry, man. I don't know what to say."

"You don' hafta talk. I gotta figure out arrangements, figure out what to do with poor Grace. She took it real hard."

Daw reached over and touched the old farmer's shoulder and Jacob bowed his head, almost driving them off the road. They drove on in silence, Jacob's jaw clenched so tight that Daw thought he might break some teeth. In town they visited the bank and Jacob handed over an envelope containing a neat stack of fifty-dollar bills.

"So, where ya gonna go from here?" Jacob asked.

"Somewhere south, maybe the Central Coast where the Pacific isn't too far away. They should be picking grapes right about now."

"There's a Greyhound station two blocks down. I think there's a morning bus headed that-a-way."

"Thanks, Jacob, for the work. Thank Joy for all the great cooking. And tell Grace to...hell I don't know what to tell her. But she's going to need help."

"Yeah, don' I know it," Jacob said and smiled. "You shoulda seen her before you showed up."

Dawson hefted his rucksack onto a shoulder. "Well, good luck and my condolences."

He moved off slowly, the morning already hot and humid, the memory of what he'd done to his fiancée's Jody fresh in his mind. He knew he could never stop drifting.

About the author:

Terry Sanville lives in San Luis Obispo, California with his artist-poet wife (his in-house editor) and two plump cats (his in-house critics). He writes full time, producing stories, essays, and novels. His stories have been accepted more than 580 times by journals, magazines, and anthologies including *The American Writers Review*, *Bryant Literary Review*, and *Shenandoah*. He was nominated four times for Pushcart Prizes and once for inclusion in Best of the Net anthology. Terry is a retired urban planner and an accomplished jazz and blues guitarist—who once played with a symphony orchestra backing up jazz legend George Shearing.

THIRD PLACE

IN THE NIGHT
©2025 by Christine Roy

The heavy, carved wooden door to Edwin James's bedroom creaked open, just for a fleeting second. Edwin kept his alert eyes hidden behind thin lids. It was one o'clock in the morning and he was awake. Again. Always.

The sound of his wife, Audrey, tapping in Mary Jane heels down the marble floor of the upper wing corridor hit him like rifle fire. His breaths shot out rapid and shaky like those of an infirm man. Only there was nothing wrong with him except for the unending battles in his mind.

He was young enough to live, to make a stand, fight for his wife. He just didn't know how to. Not anymore.

Though entombed in his chambers, too far away to hear, somewhere in the mansion a door opened, and Audrey escaped into the freedom of night. With bobbed hair, crimped and shining, dressed in sleeveless silk, she floated away, a delicate, beautiful moth of a woman.

Restlessness crept up his body. Scuttling out of bed, he shoved his feet into the soft comfort of leather opera slippers. He reached for the black velvet robe draped over the chair at his desk. Slipping the garment over his pajamas, his fingers brushed against the smooth texture of the fabric. The sensation served as a tether, something to keep him in the present. His gaze darted around the chamber, gathering details: the clock, paintings, a glass of water, the ghost. No dirt, no fear, just sadness. He breathed out, trying to steady himself, to keep his mind from traveling beyond the ornate Santa Barbara mansion perched on a bluff above the blue Pacific to the underground trenches of war.

He was home. It was over.

They'd always had separate bedrooms. At the end of the Great War in 1918, Edwin returned home from Germany a few weeks shy of his twenty-fourth birthday, with fits and night terrors. When he married Audrey Dalton one year later, his nocturnal screaming was not something he wanted to expose his beautiful, flaxen-haired bride to.

He'd tried to be normal again, to forget being buried alive, of seeing the terror in the eyes of the men, the boys, who'd died by his hand or the children who scrambled over dead bodies, screaming as they tried to pull their loved ones back to life. Except, the trauma was in him, strong and unrelenting.

He and Audrey had almost made it as a couple, as a family. For a while, focus pulled, drawn in hope and joy to a life outside themselves. Only, with the loss of their infant son, Theo, in the night's calm three years ago, grief grew between them like a chasm. Their sorrow, separate and closed, shone a harsh light upon the truth.

They were strangers, weighed down and mute to their loss.

Edwin had been a successful screenwriter, promising, funny. Directors had tried to drag him in front of the camera, fixated by the structure of his face. He'd just smile and distract them with a joke.

Though his heart still beat, the carefree young man he once was perished beside the corpses of his friends, pierced, and broken by the collapsed earth.

Some of his fellow soldiers had feared open fire or bayonets. For Edwin, terror lay in their self-made tombs, the trenches, always threatening to give way under the weight of the seemingly endless line of tanks rolling over the lives held within their sodden embrace. He'd lived in horror, imagining being swallowed and crushed by the ground hundreds of times before it actually happened.

Now he was a pale, scarred shell of a man, riddled with dark stories that slithered through his veins, unspoken and unbearable. His voice, his truth, lay buried. While others like Hemingway could touch their memories of war, drawing upon them and transforming them into literary brilliance, Edwin was but a ghost haunting his own life.

His wife was still young, a grey-eyed creature with a curious, kind nature. She could still have a life. Without him.

He just had to be brave enough to let her go.

"How long do you think?" Bertram asked, his newspaper rustling, disturbing the quiet. "How long until you say something? Put a stop to it?"

Edwin turned to the figure sitting in the armchair, dressed in the style of the last decade, waistcoat, double-breasted jacket. The handlebar mustache was still dark beneath his long, straight nose, though the hair on his head had dared to recede a bit.

Whether Bertram was a ghost or a hallucination was unknown to him. When Bertram was alive, Edwin called him father.

It happened while Edwin was away, fighting to survive among disease, rats, and mind-, shattering violence. Sitting in a trench, drinking precious words from home, he learned that his fifty-six-year-old father had died from an attack on his heart in the estate's library.

Edwin blamed himself. He wasn't there to ease the worry, prevent the strain.

"There's nothing to stop, Bertram," he stated, touching the silver-framed photograph of Audrey and Theo on his desk. "The die is cast."

"You're all wet, son," the older man scoffed. "Nothing's ever too late until it really is. I would know. You're alive and so is she. Join Audrey, Edwin. Help her."

"Ha," he scoffed. "I should dress, climb in my roadster and scour downtown Santa Barbara, sniffing like a hound dog in search of my wayward wife?"

"And how," Bertram boomed. "Toss on your glad rags and make a stand, Edwin. Show Audrey you're still here. She's looking for you in the bottom of a speakeasy glass, on crowded dance floors, in the embrace of a stranger. It's you she's trying to find again."

"But I'm here," Edwin shook his head, pacing. "Always. I don't even go to the studios anymore. I just send them pages of drivel about vamps and sheiks, and they eat it up. Plaster it across a screen at some picture palace." Disgust, anger twisted in his gut. He'd grown tired of swimming in shallow, vapid waters.

It wasn't just him. Society was playing, pretending, wrapping truth, loss and pain in witty banter and pretty fabric. The war had destroyed the world. They were just pretending it didn't.

"I understand that you're unhappy—changed." Bertram tossed the paper aside and stood. "But are you alone in that? I don't think what you fear is true. Not all of it. I would reflect on it. Don't you imagine nights would be hard for Audrey as well? Heck, even I hear them, the phantom cries of the child. Surely the mother does as well. It wasn't fair. There was no reason for little Theo's passing. It just happened."

A tremor crossed beneath Edwin's feet. The faint rumble, real and near, shook his unsettled mind. His slippered feet scuffed to the door, his shaking arm reaching to the doorframe for strength. The earth's rumble was gone from the air, but it travelled on within his mind, exposing flashing images like a picture film. Grey skies and muddy trenches filled with blood and bones washed over him.

"Edwin, Edwin," Bertram's voice echoed around him. *In* him? He wasn't sure of anything, really. "It's nothing, son. Just our old earth having a bit of grumble with us."

The ground shook again as if a train were passing close by. Edwin pushed out into the hallway, his frantic eyes on the ceiling, searching for cracks, waiting for the plaster to shed powdery dust upon him. Nothing. There was nothing wrong with the ceilings, the mansion. Yet dirt fell in his eyes, clogging his airways with memories.

Sweating and shaking, he rushed down the stairway, his slippers flying off as he sped past the confused, awakened staff.

Ignoring voices, real and filled with concern, he turned and bolted down the long, white marble hall. He held back a scream as his hands pushed upon the heavy oak of the massive doors to the outside. Terrified, he stood transfixed. It was just a door, crafted and functional. He could get past it. It was not a rough-hewn beam collapsing down upon him from an artillery blast. No one would grip his hand as they lay dying, impaled by a spear of splintered wood.

He fled into the moonlit night, his feet grabbing at the wet grass beneath him. Scrambling down the stone stairs to the sea, he inhaled deeply of the salty, free air.

The earth had stilled. All was fine. Yet, fragments of thoughts, freed by Bertram's truthful words and the snap of the past, tumbled within him now like shrapnel. Exhausted, he fell upon the sand, comforted by the grains pushing against the scars on his face.

Amidst the hazy beams of sun drifting into the formal, paneled dining room, Edwin sat gazing upon his wife as she was an oddity from the circus instead of a stunning woman in a slate-blue frock. A straw, wide-brimmed hat adorned with silk flowers lay to the side of her on the table. Her appearance, while still modern and fresh, was soft, reminiscent of a different time.

The sight of her brought tears to his eyes.

It was odd to be breakfasting together. He, in blue pinstripes, polished Italian shoes upon feet that had trod bare upon the sand just scant hours prior. She, his wife, the only woman he'd ever loved, demur and refined after a night spent God knows where.

He raised his spoon to the soft-boiled egg resting in its pressed-glass cup. As he tapped against the shell, the slight noise echoed loudly in his head. His heartbeat quickened and his mouth dried. Abandoning sustenance, he reached for his coffee and gulped down the bitter, hot liquid, trying to drown the words climbing up his throat. He had to stay quiet, let it go, keep up the façade. Nervous, he straightened his tie and coughed.

"Are you well, Edwin?" Audrey lay her toast upon her plate and looked up at him behind a swoop of ethereal bangs.

"Right as rain. Everything's jake," he lied, looking away. He kept his words bound, corded, strained. He shouldn't have, but he dared turn back, for she was like a beautiful sunset, slipping away. "You look pretty," he remarked.

"Thank you, dear. You look tired," she responded, her gaze thoughtful. "Did you sleep?"

"Ah, a little, not really," he stammered. Night was a dangerous subject. "I don't know, Audrey," he whispered. "I don't know." He pushed his hand through his hair, remembering the earth's tremors. They shot through him again, dislodging thoughts. His fingers curled into a fist that slammed down upon the table, upsetting the delicate porcelain settings.

"Edwin!" Audrey gasped, the color running from her cheeks.

As if hearing their cue, the help cleared from the room.

He looked up, staring at the vibrant designs painted onto the cream canvas-covered ceiling. The fabric was used to hide imperfections, to stabilize the plaster when shifts occurred. He wished for a similar substance to come over him, smoothing, strengthening, hiding the crumbling matter of his being.

He lowered his head and let the tremors tear it all down.

"Is he nice, Audrey?" he asked, traitorous tears slipping from his eyes. He stared at his wife, seeing the girl he'd left at the train station, the woman who waited, pledging her life to his, the despondent mother, collapsed on the floor desperate to find life in her infant son. "Please tell he's a nice man. A good man."

"What? Who..." she rose from the table abruptly, knocking her hat to the floor. "I don't know what..." she backed away. "What are you asking me, Edwin?" She shook her head, tears streaming down her face. "No one is nice, Edwin. No one is you."

"Are you happy?" He stood, taking careful steps toward her.

"No," she laughed. "I'm not happy, Edwin. I'm not sure I'm

meant to be happy." She stepped toward the window, the circular rose garden in bloom just beyond the panes of glass.

He didn't need to look to see the small statue in the middle. The little angel.

"He would have been four years old next week, Edwin," she said, looking over her shoulder. "Did you know that?"

"Yes," he said, his voice quiet as he touched her shoulder lightly. "Yes, I did."

"I relive it, Edwin, every night," she twisted away from the window, from him. Pain etched into her delicate face. "I don't know that I can do this anymore. Memories creep into the day. I'm so lonely here, without you. I understand, Edwin, truly, I do. But it's too much."

At two in the morning, Edwin sat with Bertram in the library. At their backs were hundreds of bound leather volumes: Dante, Homer, Dickens, Voltaire. Influential writers, genuine writers, not like him. Before them, the heavy red curtains carved with art deco designs flowed open to the night.

Audrey had been so pleased with the installation of the draperies. She loved putting a modern twist on the overly ornate home he'd inherited. Early on, they'd talked for hours about their love for simplistic design and what their dream home would look like if they could ever step away from the stewardship of the estate.

Edwin watched the cases being loaded into the round doors of the Rolls-Royce, stealing one last glimpse of Audrey. Her light hair glowed silver in the moon's light. There was a slight wind. Her gown of red and gold draped so elegantly upon her shoulders, blew behind her dramatically as the slit in the front revealed a flash of leg.

Out of all the horrors he'd witnessed, seeing her leave was the worst.

"Do you think the scars on your face make a difference?" Bertram asked beside him. "They don't. You're still handsome. She still loves you. But marks within, well that's a different story. They steal your life away."

"It doesn't matter, Father. It's done and over." His body was so tired, but his eyes remained open. He wondered how long a person could live without sleep; how long would it take to end it all?

The car, a New Phantom, rolled away, the sloped back looking very much like a beetle, the circular red taillights shining like a demon's eyes in the night.

He sat shaking, his insides twisting, so buried with grief he could not move, speak. Perhaps he would remain there forever, like Theo's little statue.

Another tremor like the night before shook the house, but he didn't even flinch. Minutes later, the lights went out. He welcomed the darkness.

"What would you do, Edwin?" Bertram began after hours passed wide-eyed in silence. "If you were free from this home, from the job of managing the estate, what would you do? I know you are not keen on writing for the pictures—for Hollywood."

"I don't know." Edwin hadn't thought about living anywhere else for a long time. The house was all he had left of Bertram and of Theo. Only it wasn't for the living anymore. "I had a friend in my company overseas. His name was Brian Thomas Campbell. He died next to me, the story of his homeland on his lips, of the Isle of Skye in western Scotland. I used to dream of walking the land of his stories, of living a small life in a place of great beauty and freedom."

"Dreams are good, son. Remember that." Bertram rose. "It's time to go outside now, Edwin."

"No," he said, shaking his head. "I'll think I'll stay here."

"Do one last thing for me, will you?" Bertram persisted. "Walk out the doors with your old father. Let's enjoy a sunrise, for old time's sake."

Sighing, he stood and followed Bertram's shadowy figure through the halls to the front doors. They were just past the threshold when the sharp jolt hit. Edwin staggered to the lawn in shock as the ground rolled violently beneath him and seconds seemed to shake into hours. The staff rushed from the building, some still in their nightclothes, their screams carrying on the wind.

Though his heart lurched in his chest as his eyes fell upon the sight of the mansion's limestone crumbling to the ground in a sickening roar, his mind was strangely present. He looked to Bertram as the area of the building containing the library collapsed upon itself in a heap of roaring destruction.

"You saved me," he said to the increasingly transparent man. "Did you know, Father?"

"Live your life, Edwin. Any way you want," Bertram said, smiling. His blue eyes glowed brighter and brighter as he faded into the smoky air.

Choking on dust, Edwin stumbled toward the kind, loyal staff huddled in a terrified group. His words were clear, his mind free, as he offered them assurances and a plan of action.

Having the wherewithal to remember the tents and supplies stored in the relatively unscathed carriage house, their makeshift camp near the long rectangular lotus pond stood erected and operational just hours later. Taking a sip of water from a bucket filled at the still-working old well pump, he glanced at the two white swans swimming side by side in the pond, unfazed, untouched. Beautiful. Suddenly overcome with drowsiness, he rubbed his sleepy eyes and lay down on his cot.

His eyes were still half open when he saw his wife coming toward him. She had no shoes on, and the long layer of her red and gold dress dragged behind her like a mermaid's tail. Her hair stuck out wildly around her head and cuts and smudges marred her face. She knelt beside him, laying her head upon his chest.

"I thought I might have died under the rubble of the speakeasy," she spoke to the birdsong air. "I don't think my body would ever have been found. Rumors would have flown when someone who looked so similar to me would be spotted, say, in Argentina or Monaco. But..." she raised herself up on her palms above him, her grey eyes shining, "as luck would have it, I climbed out from the destruction relatively unscathed with only one desire intact—to see you, Edwin. As the world shook and everything crumbled and died

around me, I just wanted to see you again. My beautiful husband."
She kissed his lips, her salty tears falling upon him like drops of
rain.

"Is there room for me, Edwin, on your little cot?" she whispered,
her eyes fearful.

He sat up, taking her face in his hands, and kissed her forehead,
his fingers brushing away the grime from her delicate face.

"Yes, Audrey," he responded, pulling her to him. "Always and
forever."

About the author:

A native of rural Connecticut, Christine Roy grew up surrounded
by history and haunted tales. While her educational background is
in communications, her writing often follows the path of the
paranormal. On this journey, she has completed three novels and is
continuing on with a variety of new projects. In recent times, she
has found publication as the winner of a Bardsy contest with her
short story "Holiday Spirit" and with Writer's Playground for
"Playing for Sam."

KNIGHT FALL
©2025 by Joseph J. Salerno

Amelia's mother hired a man in his mid-twenties to spend early Wednesday evenings during the autumn semester playing chess and having take-out dinners with her teenage daughter. Amelia was partially blind from an early-childhood brain infection, and she loved to play the game, both on her computer and with others on her large, brightly lit actual chessboard. The young man, a graduate student at the local university, was quite an expert on the subject and had been hired to teach the finer points.

"What kind of name is Springer Daniels?" Amelia inquired at their first meeting. "I mean, *Springer Daniels*? Really? Do you ever get called a springer spaniel?"

"Yes, of course," he replied. "Springer spaniel, springer doodle, Jerry Springer, Daniel Boone. All sorts of names."

At the outset, Amelia felt a bit over-entitled, as it were, to have this weekly instructor. Despite her visual impairment (seeing only shadows in her right eye, having severe myopia in her left), she was a sophomore at the local district high school, and she attended regular classes. She had recently joined the chess club and displayed a high aptitude for it. Upon learning of this, Amelia's widowed mother decided to hire this Springer Daniels fellow for the time period of her weekly art class when she'd be absent from home.

Amelia felt grateful, but thought, *Chess instructor? Who is this guy?*

Springer Daniels—*Spree* to his friends—was a jovial, spontaneous twenty-six-year-old living with some internal conflicts and contradictions. Attending the local university for an advanced degree in mathematics and computer science, he was just as likely to spend days at the out-of-state sky-diving school as he was spending a week at the even-farther-out Buddhist Ashram, meditating and chanting "OMs." A chess maven and junior master, he would often unwind and relax with a rowdy and boisterous game of Backgammon, cursing and screaming at the dice. Although usually a hyper rational young man, he sometimes loved to roleplay into depths of vulgar rants. And, despite being in love with his high school sweetheart, his current fiancée, he would often cheat on her. Simply because he could.

"Oh, man," Amelia sighed after they had played their first game together. "You pretty much wiped me out. Where'd ya learn to play?"

"My father was a chess master, and *he* was the son of a chess master. From Poland. You did okay, just brought out your queen too early. A fairly common mistake." It had been an entertaining game for him. Despite her loss, he was impressed by the skill of the fifteen-year-old.

"Hmm, yeah. My mother said we should play two matches, one pre-prandial and one post-prandial. What would you like for dinner?" She handed him two take-out menus. "Chinese or Italian?"

They ordered in some Chinese food, had dinner, and then played a second game. Amelia played much better than in the first, showing her new mentor her true aptitude.

"So far, you are an excellent instructor," she told him.

"Hooh, boy! I can't be *that* good, not *this* quickly. But it's nice to know I'm swimming with a shark. Next week, I bring my A-Game."

Over the next few Wednesdays, it was Amelia's sensibility and style of play that intrigued the young man. Beside her seemingly innate feel for mid-game and even end-game strategy, her tactile actions fascinated him. Perhaps due to her visual impairment, Amelia would often pick up the chess piece she was about to move and feel its distinct contours with her fingertips. Entire minutes caressing the queen's crown, the bishop's miter, the knight's horse-snout and mane...

"Does the name 'Springer' have any meaning or significance?" she abruptly asked one evening.

"Yeah," he replied. "It actually means *knight*, or something akin to *jumping horse*, in old German. As I said, my dad was a chess master."

"It seems appropriate," she said, "the knight being able to spring over and jump to avoid other pieces. Do you consider yourself a knight of sorts?"

"I consider myself your chess instructor. I consider some of your questions to be rude and a bit too personal. *and*, considering that you are losing this one, big time, I am not surprised."

"Hmmm."

After five Wednesdays of instruction, Amelia informed Springer that she was participating in a chess tournament the upcoming Saturday. She asked for a general assessment of her play.

"Well," he told her, "you often lose patience with the center of the board, make mistakes there. And, when playing black, you get too restrained and reactive. Otherwise, Amelia, I think you got game."

"Okay. Understood. Italian tonight?"

"Sure," he said. "How about a few rounds of Backgammon over dinner?"

And so, along with a few chicken parm heroes, they interrupted the chess instruction with a few games of Backgammon. Springer insisted, as was his strange policy, that they be both vocal and vulgar while rolling the dice.

"What the f---!" she yelled, imitating his prompts. "I needed a freaking three! Just one stinking three! What am I supposed to do with this damn double five?!?"

"Dammit!" he groaned, after his roll. "I missed both your lousy stinking blots! How is that even possible?"

"No sixes on these pukey-shit dice! Springer, are they loaded? Did you load these dice?"

Besides playing some games of what he'd dubbed "Vulgar

Backgammon," Springer often used the dinner interlude to call his fiancée, Nadine, and to touch base with some friends on late-hour plans. Amelia, in listening, was fascinated and even a bit envious of his social circle and wondered if she'd be able to enjoy a similar one in coming years.

The following week, her report to him on the tournament was mixed. Although Amelia had won her individual match, her team did poorly as a whole. A true sport, she told Springer she wished it were otherwise.

"We can only hold up *our* corner of the universe," he consoled her. "I'm proud of you."

Their first game of chess that evening was interrupted by a cell phone spat between Springer and his fiancée. When he'd returned his attention to the board, he instructed Amelia on the nuances of inching forward pawns with purpose and patience.

"Does Nadine know you're cheating on her with her younger sister?" Amelia ventured.

Springer Daniels threw up his arms, slapped the sides of his head, and let out a "*Hah!*" He and his student looked at each other without expression. "*That*, my dear Amelia, is out of line. I can sit here and instruct you about Ruy Lopez and aggressiveness and restraint and Sicilian defenses and pawn positioning, but I *cannot* instruct you on how *not* to pay attention to other people's conversations."

"You know, Spree, you ought to keep in mind that *you* are never the *only* knight on the board."

A simple numerical notation occurred in Springer's mind. He was twenty-six years old, and he was talking to a fifteen-year-old. When the hell did this teenager become an old savant?

"Are you going to complain to my mother about me?" she asked. "I find our meetings valuable and...enlightening. I'd hate for them to end because of my...I dunno..."

"No, I will file no complaint," he assured her. "I suppose some of my instruction should be about discretion, on my part as much as yours. Let's call this game a draw, order some Chinese. Maybe play some Backgammon."

"Yes."

Over a dish of Moo Goo Gai Pan, in the middle of a game of Backgammon, Springer rolled a double six when he needed a low roll.

"F..ing shit! What is it with these bullshit dice? I need a double six like I need a third armpit, or a freaking overly inquisitive teenager."

And as she rolled a five two, she shouted "Yes! That's my roll! I mean like, no shit! I hit two of your blots. Two pieces back on the bar for the freaking two-timing finagler!"

He frowned as he rolled the dice. The combination was not good enough to re-enter his bits.

"Hmmm, no damn inroads, on the board, *or* in teaching you discretion."

She rolled another advantageous combination. "Patience, good Knight. Patience."

"Hey, Spree," said Amelia on a later Wednesday, "you were once nice enough to tell me what *your* name means. Can I tell you about mine?"

"Sure. I'm all ears."

"Well, like your name, *Amelia* is also of Germanic origin. It means *vigorous work*. I was named after that aviator from the 1930s, the one who disappeared flying over the Pacific."

"That's a...brave name. From, and *for*, a brave young woman."

"Yeah. Brave. I sometimes feel that my mother wishes that I would disappear."

"Oh, stop. Your mother loves you," said Springer. "Self-pity does not become you. And you've got talent. I mean, so far, you're winning this damn game. Oops! The vulgarity should be reserved for the Backgammon."

"Yes, of course." She looked down at the board with a sad look on her face. "This is chess. It is genteel. It is highbrow. It is dignified. Are we *serious* with all this?"

"Not...totally. But mostly. Your, uh, conscientiousness toward the game reflects your dedication to excellence. To goodness and discipline in life. To your, uh, *vigorous work* ethic. Ahh, Amelia, there will always be a time for a game of Vulgar Backgammon. So, what's the deal? Are we having Italian tonight?"

"No. No Italian. No Chinese. A friend of Mother's is dropping off some fine Scottish fare. Which do you prefer? A Quarter Pounder, or a Big Mac?"

"Hmmm."

Amelia's autumn semester was drawing to a close, and in an early December chess tournament, she led her team to first place. A week later, her mother informed her that Springer had completed his degree program, and that the upcoming Wednesday would be the last week of instruction.

That final evening, they played a casual and non-competitive game. She made him some special herbal tea. They talked. He asked her what she planned on doing with her life. She said she was interested in medicine or psychology. He said it was still early for her, but he was happy that she was thinking about it.

When he started talking about how excited yet nervous he was about his new job in Silicon Valley, three thousand miles away, she whispered to him, "Please, don't talk."

The young, partially blind teenager lifted her small soft hands and slowly and delicately put her fingertips to her mentor's face. She lightly touched his ears and lobes, his chin, his cheeks, his nose. She felt his hair between her fingertips, then gently felt his eyes, the brows and the closed lashes.

"Of course, I think it should go without saying, I will always love you, Springer Daniels."

On opening his eyes, he held her wrists and pushed her hands back to her. "In matters of chess and school, I think, Amelia, that you are brilliant. But in this matter of you and me, you're a stupid kid."

"Ohh, Spree... Were you *born* a slimy bastard? Or did you just *become* one?"

"What's the diff?" he replied. "The fish is in the water, and the water's in the fish. I love you too, Amelia. Maybe in about six or eight years, you can look me up. But, anyway, I see truly blue horizons for you."

Amelia's mother found them in the living room at the gaming

table, just talking and finishing their cups of tea. After having handed him his last paycheck, she asked Springer his final impressions of her daughter.

"Wonderful kid," he said. "Truly. I hope I have served her well."

"And Amelia," asked her mother, "what would you say are your final impressions of Mr. Springer Daniels?"

The young lady took a last sip of tea, put down her cup, and stood. She looked at her mentor one final time, and she silently placed her fingertips to her lips. Without adieu, she quietly walked upstairs and disappeared for the night.

About the author:

Joseph Salerno works as a part-time office manager for a small accounting firm. He has a BA in Psychology from SUNY—Empire State College and he is a proud member of the Long Island Writers' Guild.

His stories have been published on numerous occasions: Guilders '84—The Literary Magazine of Hostra University (1984), Open Minds Quarterly (2014), and Scribes Valley Publishing anthologies 2019-2025.

Joseph is an enthusiastic board game player (quite ruthless at Backgammon), and he lives with about a dozen large houseplants three blocks from the New York City limits.

NUMBERS ON A SCREEN
©2025 by Dominik Slusarczyk

Chapter 1

The rage builds inside Becky like a fire heaving itself towards the heavens. As she turns to Lilly her fingers clench into a fist momentarily but then she checks herself and remembers who Lilly is and what she means to her. Her fingers return to hanging limply at her side.

"You're wrong," she says. "You're always wrong. You were wrong about David, about Simon. You're wrong about Ben too: he isn't with me because of my money."

"That's all they want, Becks," Lilly says. "All anybody sees when they look at you is your bank balance."

"What am I supposed to do? I want love, Lilly. Everyone wants love. Everyone wants marriage and kids. Everyone wants to find the one person they were meant to be with, the person god created just for them. I want that too. I want love. I want a wedding with a five-tiered cake and a band playing my favourite songs. I want you to cry halfway through your maid of honour speech. I want to fall in love, Lilly. Billionaires need people just as much as poor people do."

"It's obvious what he's after, Becks: you've only been together a couple of months and he's already talking about marriage. All he wants is half your money. You'll find the right person, Becks, but that person is not Ben."

Becky turns from her and walks to the ornate wall surrounding the balcony they are stood on. The wall is a flat slab of marble held up by rounded pillars that bulge at the bottom but are thin at the top. Becky leans her hands on the wall and stares out over the village spread out below her. The buildings are so small they can surely only house children. Smoke curls up from every chimney because the villagers have to burn vast fires to keep the winter at bay. Beyond the village is the forest that the villagers have fought tooth and nail to keep logging companies away from, and beyond the forest are the mountains—great peaks so vast that some of them stretch high above the clouds.

"They always talk about marriage," Becky says with a sigh. "I had a boy bring up marriage on the first bloody date once. They all look deep into my eyes and tell me they've never felt this way about someone. Why not get married, they say. We could do it right now: there's a chapel on the corner."

"They're making it easy for you," Lilly says. "You know the ones who talk about marriage are the ones who aren't worth keeping around."

Lilly walks to Becky and puts her hand on her back. On Lilly's wrist is a bracelet that glitters with diamonds and emeralds and her fingers are covered with glittering rings—years' worth of birthday presents from Becky.

"You need to date someone who's already rich," Lilly says. "If you marry another billionaire, you'll know they're not after you for your money because they've already got loads of money themselves."

"All the other billionaires are old and ugly. It takes most people decades to make billions. Why'd I have to be stupid and go and do it by twenty-three?"

"You'll find someone, Becks. God made someone for everyone."

They go inside and drink some cocktails. When Becky has drunk enough that she has courage she rings Ben and breaks up with him. She sees his true colours. He shouts and screams and calls her a whore. He says he's going to hire lawyers to get the money 'that is rightfully his'. At the end of the phone call, he threatens Becky. He says he will find her and hurt her if she doesn't put five hundred million in his account right now. Becky hangs up. She isn't worried about the threat of violence: she pays bodyguards so she doesn't have to worry about stuff like that.

Becky and Lilly continue drinking. At around midnight Becky cries because she is single and alone. Lilly hugs her and tells her that she isn't alone because she has Lilly. Becky says it isn't the same. Lilly doesn't respond because she knows what Becky says is true.

Becky wakes up in bed with no memory of how she got there. Her head is pounding like there is an army marching to war inside of it and her mouth is so dry it is like she has eaten a handful of sawdust. Becky groans, rolls over, and thinks about going back to sleep before she realises her need for water is so great she will not be able to sleep until she has drunk something. She gingerly climbs out of bed and wraps a fluffy red dressing gown around her naked body. She stumbles to the door that is almost twice her height yet still doesn't reach the ceiling. The door is decorated with thin lines of real gold curled into leaves and other pretty designs.

The door swings open easily even though it is vast and heavy. As she walks through the living room decorated with tall marble pillars, she spots Lilly stretched out on one of the sofas. They must have been very drunk indeed last night: the house has twenty bedrooms so there is never any need to sleep on a sofa.

Becky fills a pint glass with water from the tall tap. The second the liquid touches her lips she starts to feel better. She gulps the whole pint down in seconds and her head starts to throb slightly less. She fills the glass up again but only manages to drink half of it the second time. She pours the rest of the glass down the sink and heads back to her bedroom. Her bare fleet slap on the cold floor. As she passes through the room outside her bedroom, she sees Lilly sat up on the edge of the sofa with her head in her hands.

"Morning," Becky croaks. Lilly glances up for a second then she returns her head to her hands. All Lilly can manage in response to Becky's greeting is a quiet groan.

"Go get in one of the beds, you fool," says Becky quietly. Lilly tries to glance up again but fails. Becky isn't sure if Lilly has the strength to make it to one of the bedrooms with how hungover she looks.

Becky crawls into her bed and pulls the fluffy duvet up to her chin. She drifts off to sleep immediately. She dreams of Ben. It is their wedding day. They are stood in front of the priest at the front of the church. The priest is small and overweight. His green robes flow all around him. There is a huge bald patch on the top of his head and the hair that remains around the sides of his head is light grey. Becky is barely listening to him recite the Mass. Her eyes are staring straight into Ben's. She sees a look she doesn't like there; it is a look of lust, greed, and he is smiling so widely that his cheeks look fat and ugly like he has stuffed them full of food. Becky wakes with a start, and suddenly all of her worries are gone. She is glad she broke up with Ben. She is glad she didn't marry him. It is likely that he didn't even find her attractive.

Becky feels much better now: her headache is only a murmur, and she feels far livelier. She gets out of bed and dresses in a t-shirt and jeans, both light grey. When she exits her bedroom, she sees Lilly sat on the sofa, eating breakfast.

"There's some bacon left in the pan," Lilly says when she sees Becky.

Becky walks straight into the kitchen and finds the pan Lilly was talking about. She makes a sandwich and then she goes back into the living room Lilly is in. As they eat, they discuss what they are going to do today and they have already made plans to go to the zoo when Becky remembers she has to go to a stupid board meeting.

An hour later Becky's driver tells her they have to leave in ten minutes. Becky has to rush to be ready in time. She can't be late: she owns the company so they can't start the meeting without her. Whenever Becky is late the other board members have to sit around waiting for her to arrive. Becky is always embarrassed when she walks in and sees everyone else sat around playing on their phones.

Lilly says she will stay in the house and watch films or something until Becky gets back. Lilly has her own house a mile away, which

Becky bought for her, but she barely spends any time there. Becky and Lilly have been friends since the first day of primary school. Becky sometimes thinks how different her life would have been if the teacher had sat her next to someone else instead of Lilly. It was Lilly's idea to start the business. Without Lilly, Becky would probably be working in McDonalds or a call centre or something. But the teacher *did* sit them next to each other, and now Becky is the fourth richest person in the world.

Becky's company's headquarters is in the centre of the nearest city. It is an hour's drive away and Becky knows she should probably live closer but there are simply no properties in the city nice enough for someone like her. She owned a flat right at the top of a skyscraper for a couple of years, but it was too small and she hated it. She guesses the commute isn't too bad. She only has to do it once a week. Becky's company basically runs itself; or, rather, the people Becky is paying to run it, run it for her. All she has to do is attend one meeting a week where she has to make a couple of decisions. They are all the most important decisions, of course, and Becky does her small job well, as the company's growing value proves.

Everyone else stops chatting as soon as Becky enters the boardroom. Most people have drinks in their hands. There are whiskeys and coffees in equal measure. They ask Becky to decide whether to build a factory in India or China, then she has to decide whether to make their new phone red or blue. She decides to build factories in *both* India and China and she decides to make phones in not only red *and* blue but yellow as well. It somehow takes three hours to make those decisions so by the time the meeting is over Becky is tired and bored. Everyone else on the board stays sat in their chairs until Becky has left the room.

When Becky gets home, Lilly is dozing on the same sofa she slept on last night. Becky shakes her gently to wake her up. Lilly opens the eye closest to Becky an inch.

"Oh, Becks," Lilly groans. "Why'd you wake me? I was dreaming of the most beautiful beach."

"What's the point of dreaming about a beach? If you want to go to a beach, let's just go to a beach."

They hire their own private island just off the coast of Spain. The mansion on the island is beautiful but they both agree that the mansion they own is way nicer.

Chapter 2

"The stock is falling at a tremendous rate," Mr Potkins, the CEO of Becky's company, says. "Are you still determined not to sell? If you sold now, you'd get billions. In a month...who knows? In a month there might not be a company left to sell."

"We aren't interested in selling," Lilly says. Her blond hair is tied into the ponytail she always wears in the board room. She is wearing a beautiful light grey suit with a bright red tie underneath it.

"Yeah," Becky says. She is sat next to Lilly at the head of the table. Her short brown hair barely comes down past her ears. She is wearing a t-shirt and shorts, both grey. "It's only a little recession, Potkins. We'll be fine: our company is too big to fail."

"That's what the banks said, Becky, and look at them now. Bankrupt. Broken. Can't even afford to pay their wages this month."

"Tech is different," Lilly says. "People love new phones, new computers. People might not have enough money to buy new tech right now, but they will in a couple of months. All we have to do is wait for the stock market to go back up."

"Look," Mr Potkins says. "Our expenses are bigger than our earnings. We must..."

"We'll just get another government grant," Becky says. "The government love handing out money to rich people; it's their favourite game."

Lilly nods her head. She knows all about the government grants: she was the one who made the phone call about it a couple of days ago.

Mr Potkins frowns but he does not voice any more objections. They move on to discussing other matters. Less than a week later the government gives their company twenty billion, almost double what they asked for. The money is more than enough to last until the stock market rebounds and goes back to where it was before the recession. The recession only lasted six months but millions of people lost their jobs in that time. Hundreds of thousands of people were made homeless. When the recession ends, half of the twenty billion the government gave them is still in their bank account.

Becky and Lilly start constructing a new mansion. They want to live somewhere warmer. They buy an island off the coast of Greece. The island is small but every edge of it is a beautiful sandy beach. They build a mansion four times as big as the mansion they are currently living in. It has tennis courts, cinemas, pools of all shapes and sizes which will never get used because they can just swim in the sea. They start joking about how their current mansion is a poor people's mansion, but they never joke in front of the help who might take it the wrong way.

Their company continues to grow. Soon they are making tablets as well as phones, then, only a couple of months later, they make their first games console. The games console is a huge success. By the time the new mansion is finished, Becky is the second richest person in the world. Lilly has no money of her own.

They have to hire twice as many people as they did in the poor people's mansion to make sure the new mansion runs smoothly. They have a team of cooks, a team of cleaners. They have so many bodyguards, they had to build the bodyguards their own mansion behind the main mansion. Becky forces the rest of the board to fly out so they can hold the board meetings on the island. Lilly always sits next to Becky at the head of the table. They make all of the major decisions together. It was Lilly's idea to make a games console and now the computer games side of their business is as profitable as the phones.

"What's it all for, Lilly?" Becky asks.

"What do you mean?"

"Money. What's it for?"

"You buy things with it."

"It's a stupid system."

"We don't get to change the world, Becks: we have to follow the same rules everyone else has to follow."

"I want to do more with our money. I want our money to do more good."

"So, start a charity. We can help starving children or something."

"Maybe that is what money is for. Maybe money is for helping people."

Becky works tirelessly to set up a charity. She makes phone calls and holds meetings with all different types of people. Lilly lies on the beach and enjoys the sunshine. Six months later, Becky launches her charity. Journalists from all over the world attend the press conference where she announces the launch of her charity. She tells them she thinks money is for helping people. They roll their eyes and tell her money is for paying rent and buying food.

The charity gives starving children food and sick children medicine. When Lilly sees how many people they are helping, she gets far more interested in the charity. She starts attending the board meetings and giving her opinion on what they should do next.

"It's not a good investment," Mr Witters, the CEO of the charity, says. "We'll spend millions and only save a handful of lives. Our money would be better spent on a different project."

"We will do this project and the different project," Lilly says. "We have enough money, Witters."

"Saving a couple of lives is better than the money sitting in the bank doing nothing," Becky says. "This is what money is for, Witters: money is for helping people."

"Money is for buying cars and buying houses," Mr Witters says.

"Money is for investing," Mr Salmon, sat to Becky's left in a light brown suit, says. "You have a little bit of money, you invest it, suddenly you have more money. You use money to make more money."

"Pointless," Becky says.

"Stupid," Lilly says.

"What do you do with the money you make from your investments?" Becky asks. "Do you invest that as well? Then you have more money. What do you do with that? Invest it? Where does it end? When do you have enough money?"

"Money can buy anything, Becky," Mr Salmon says. "Money can buy cars, so you want as much money as possible so you can buy as many things as possible!

"Money is for helping people," Becky says. "We are going to help as many people as we can."

They spend years spending money on charity work. They build hospitals and hand out free medicine to everyone who shows up. They build wells so people can have fresh water, houses so people can be out of the cold.

Suddenly Becky is not the second richest person in the world anymore; suddenly she isn't even in the top ten.

People start giving them awards: the French government give them a medal, then the Egyptian government give them a fancy certificate. The newspapers talk about them all the time: they talk about the hospitals, the wells, the houses. The general public do not understand what Becky is doing at all. She is worth billions, they say. She should be helping more than she is. She should be giving away more money. There are still children starving. That is Becky's fault: she should have used her money to save them. Becky ignores the general public. She doesn't go on their forums, use their social medias. The only person whose opinion she cares about is Lilly.

It takes them twenty years to give away all of their money. They still have the island and the business, but Becky doesn't appear on any rich lists anymore. The charity expenses are so much that they completely cancel out any profit the company makes. Sometimes Becky feels a tinge of regret when she remembers how much money she used to have but whenever that happens, she thinks about how money is just a number on a bank statement which has no real significance to anyone except the people reading rich lists in newspapers.

"We can't afford it," Mr Witters says. "We only have twenty million in the bank. We can't build hospitals in Africa and hospitals in India. You have to choose, Becky. You have to choose who to save."

"Why should I be the one who chooses?" Becky says. "Why should I be responsible for who lives and who dies? If I don't build hospitals in Africa, then Africans will die, and I have blood on my hands. If I don't build hospitals in India, then Indians will die and I, again, have blood on my hands. I refuse to make this decision: I will not be responsible for people dying."

"We will build the hospitals in Africa," Lilly says. Her once blonde hair is now grey, but Becky still thinks she is the most beautiful person in the world, far more beautiful than any of the stupid boys she used to date who only wanted to take her money and hoard it themselves.

About the author:

Dominik Slusarczyk is an artist who makes everything from music to painting. He was educated at The University of Nottingham where he got a degree in biochemistry. His fiction has been published in various literary magazines including *The Raven Review* and *Odd Magazine*. His fiction came 1st in *The Cranked Anvil Short Story Competition*, 2nd in *The Streetlight Magazine Flash Fiction Contest*, and 3rd in *The Northwind Writing Award*. His full-length poetry collection *Reaction* is out now with *Cyberwit*.

WILDFLOWERS
©2025 by Lenora Salvucci

In the late '20s, right up to the mid '50s the building that now housed the Stone Hill theater was then the Stone Hill orphanage. It stood on bare earth that became mud in the rain and dust in the dry, summer heat. Then one spring a load of surplus crushed rock, left over from a nearby highway blasting project, was trucked up the hill and there was enough to cover all the dirt. That's how it came to be known as Stone Hill. After a couple of years, a generous contractor offered to tar a small square of the yard to accommodate a playground for the children. A chain link fence secured the playground. The large brick building at the top of the incline was clearly visible from the road.

John Costa, making his way up the hill to the theater now, remembered riding past the orphanage as a child. Seated next to his sister in the back seat of the Pontiac, he'd peek out at the children scampering around the yard and at the faces pressed against the fence, fingers coiled around the metal links. Sometimes a small arm would reach through the fence opening and wave at the cars driving by. Women pushed baby carriages in single file, back and forth, as if in a procession. The very word "orphan" conjured up fearful images in young John's mind and a shiver through his body, chilly as January winds. He used to wonder who they called in the middle of the night when thunder rolled, and lightning flashed. Who shook them awake out of a scary dream and showed them there was no monster in the closet or lurking under the bed? Did anyone read them stories, hug them, hear their prayers? Did anyone love them?

As the building loomed into view, John would climb into the front seat between his parents, insisting he just wanted a better view of the road ahead. The car was small, and the front seat would be cramped with the three of them, but John would pull up his knees to avoid the stick shift and wrap his arms around his shins. He didn't mind. The safety he felt sitting between his parents was worth the discomfort as his dad navigated the long, winding road ahead. John would look back over his shoulder as the distance widened between him and the orphans. The sound of their laughter always puzzled him. They *sounded* happy but how could they be? If John was one of them, he knew as certainly as he could feel the beat of his heart, that he would cry at some point every day of his life until the day he died.

That was Stone Hill Orphanage then, now Stone Hill Community Theater, where he was walking up the cement steps, where a man named Rufus Lee Wetherly was teaching eager young high school students about theater and acting. John of course could not know that was not the man's real name or that Stone Hill had once been his home back then, back in the day when it was an orphanage.

The caretaker, Lee, had been the first to hear the baby crying. He squinted into the darkness, pulling on his overalls and went barefoot from his small room in the field into the warm June night, following the whimpering sounds that led him to the front steps of the orphanage. The baby was inside a wicker basket and wrapped in a blue blanket. Lee picked up the basket and made his way back to his place, hushing the baby quiet. The baby, a boy, was stained with blood from his birth. Lee washed him gently with a piece of cloth. After patting him dry he folded a clean white sheet, placed it inside the basket and wrapped him again in the blanket. Then he hurried across the courtyard and into the big kitchen where he took a couple of diapers from the supply closet and a baby bottle that he filled with milk. Warm, dry and fed; the baby's needs were met, at least for a while.

In the morning Lee brought him to the main house, the orphanage. After careful inspection by Doc Goodwin, the baby was duly installed as a resident and given the name Joseph. Lee said the name under his breath and nodded. "God bless you, Joseph," he murmured.

Joseph may have been blessed in many ways, but his health was a liability from the start. He was sickly, given to fits of colic. Rocking seemed to be all that quieted him, but at night the resident staff was a mere skeleton crew, spread thin among so many children, and weary. So, whenever Lee offered to relieve them of their burdensome new charge, they were quite willing to give the child over to him.

After tending the grounds all day and making repairs where needed, there was not much else for Lee to do. Sure, he could spiff himself up, get himself into the city to the clubs that dotted the shabby streets behind the textile mills, listen to the jazz, maybe get himself dealt into a card game, or follow some woman down into the darkness on a creaky old bed. But on his meager wages those nights out were few and far between. Still, in those days, when even white men went begging for work, Lee considered himself a fortunate man indeed. He had a roof over his head, never mind it leaked in a few places in spite of all the patches, nothing a couple of pans couldn't handle. And he was surrounded by children who lightened his heart and made him smile, who jumped up and down clapping their hands when sometimes he returned from a trip downtown and emptied his pockets of two-for-a-penny balloons or lollipops. Stone Hill filled the hours in the day and the children filled the space in a life that was empty of a family of his own. He was luckier than most for sure.

He enjoyed being of use, outside of the job he was paid to do. It made him feel needed. He was especially taken with this new baby and reasoned it must have been because he had found him and cared for him in the first lonely hours of his life. He had washed the tiny body clean of that troublesome and troubled birth.

Sometimes it would take most of the night to quiet Joseph. Lee would settle into the big Boston rocker in the playroom and when he was sure the baby was asleep, he'd lay him in the crib but stand around a few minutes just in case, practically holding his breath. Satisfied all was well for the night, Lee would tiptoe out of the room, past the other sleeping children, and make his way outside to the small room he called home, humming the last of an old lullaby recalled from his own childhood.

It was no great secret that babies stood the best chance of being adopted and Joseph was only one of a handful. But he was usually passed over for a more rotund, animated red-cheeked baby. By the time he was three, he didn't want to be adopted and at that early age, developed his own game of pretend. He'd cough and drop his eyelids so that he looked tired and disinterested. Somebody else was always chosen and that was fine with him.

Lee called Joseph his shadow. The boy followed him around, tossing off one question after another. *What are you doing now? How do you do that? Can I help you?* As Joseph grew older the questions changed. When he was five, he asked why Lee's skin was so much darker than his own. When Lee tried to explain about race and nationality Joseph screwed up his nose and asked about his own background in a simple childlike manner. *How about me? What am I?* To which Lee could only say he was powerful sorry, he just didn't know. Then he pointed to the side of the road beyond the garden. "I 'spect you is kinda like them wildflowers over there. No one knows how they got started and why they keep growing, they just do. And I dare anyone say they're not as beautiful as these here roses that we plant ourselves."

"Wildflowers," Joseph said.

"Yep. Just as good and every bit as pretty as these here flowers."

"And I was born right here? Maybe over by that tree in the woods or out there in the open field. Do you know, Lee? Do you?"

Lee shook his head and touched the boy's cheek. "Joseph, I only know where I found you."

One day Joseph climbed over the chain link fence and wandered into the densely wooded area behind the

building where the children were not allowed. He wasn't afraid of the woods, at least not in daylight, but every few feet he checked over his shoulder to be certain the weathervane on the orphanage roof was still visible.

Dead leaves crunched under his feet, and he used a twig to move them around, searching for anything his mother may have left behind: a ribbon, a pin, a scarf. He sat down on a fallen branch, let a ladybug crawl on his hand and finger, then shook it off. He would not have minded being born in the woods in the middle of a warm night. It was quiet, peaceful except for the occasional rush of a bird or two flying out from a tree. God, he wished he had the power to recall something about her, the touch of her hand, the scent of soap or cologne, the sound of her voice, the color of her eyes. Were they blue? Or darkest brown, like his? *Mama.*

He came out of his reverie at the sound of "Hey, little boy. What're you doing wandering around these woods?" Joseph stood rigid at the sight of the police officer.

"Nothing."

"You belong over there?" gesturing with his head toward the orphanage.

Joseph nodded.

"Then come on now, back you go."

As they neared the fenced-in yard, Joseph saw Lee and Mrs. Hallowell, the woman in charge.

The policeman nodded to Joseph. "This one of yours?"

Lee nodded as the policeman lifted Joseph over the fence to him. "You might want to keep a closer watch on these kids."

A few feet away, the policeman stopped and turned around. "You say something?"

"No suh, just speaking to the boy here."

The policeman nodded slowly and walked away.

"I'm sorry, Lee"

"Well, sorry or not, Mrs. Hallowell is powerful angry."

***

He was to stay inside for the next three days. No reading, no drawing, no toys. So, he lay on his bed, his fingers laced behind his neck, listening to the children playing outside. He dozed off and on and sometime in the middle of the afternoon Lee sneaked in and handed him a piece of paper and two crayons he'd scrounged up, one red, one blue. Lee's visit cheered him until Lee advised him to give up his searching and looking for answers about his mama. "Best you face it sooner rather than later," he said. "You is an orphan, little man. That means you got no folks, no kin, and that be that. But, and this be true, it don't mean you ain't loved. Hear me now?"

Joseph tried to be brave and hold back the tears. That's when Lee told him he should let them run free lest they rust his insides. "You sad, you sad. Another day, you be happy and you smile."

In the Spring, Joseph helped Lee turn the soil in the vegetable garden, helped him plant seeds or have ready whatever tool he might need. Together they patted down mounds of earth, pulled weeds, and reaped a steady harvest right into Fall. They built a scarecrow from a couple of 2x4's, dressed it in a ragged shirt and pants and stuffed an old pillowcase with newspaper for its head.

"That's some funny looking creature," Joseph said.

"He surely is ain't he? We should give him a name."

"Give him my name 'cause I want a new one."

"Huh? Why? Joseph's a good name."

Joseph shrugged, bit into a fresh string bean and squinted into the sun. "I want a real name. First, last and all mine. One I picked myself."

Lee wiped sweat from the back of his neck and forehead. "Well, I guess you can decide that for yourself one day when you're older."

"I already decided. I want my name to be Rufus Lee Wetherly."

Lee sat down against a tree and talked through a laugh. "Well, hold on now. That name's spoken for and if you'll be excusing me, little man, I ain't quite done with it yet."

"Oh, I don't mean right now. I was thinking I could have it when you don't need it anymore. Not that I want you to be done with it, not for at least a hundred more years."

"A hundred, huh?"

Joseph nodded. "At least."

"Mmmm, yeah, well, you let old Lee think on this one. I suppose there's a chance I could pass it on to you seeing I have no children of my own...let me put some thought on it. In the meanwhile, help me with these weeds 'fore they choke all the goodness out of them Big Boy tomatoes."

When Joseph was nine, Lee thought him old enough to have the note his mother had written, the note that had been pinned to the blanket. Lee had preserved all the remnants of the boy's birth including the wicker basket. Joseph's hands trembled a bit as he unfolded the paper and went off alone to read it. He would read it many times over in the days and weeks that followed but he only needed to read it once to know for certain that he loved the woman who'd written it. He wished only to find her, to tell her that he would indeed forgive her as she had hoped he would.

Lee held him close that day, his arms tight around the thin, teary-eyed boy, "Aw, little man. You will just have to find some other way to forgive your Mama."

The well-to-do ladies and gentlemen who had embraced Stone Hill as their favorite charity, and whose donations had supplemented the city's meager allotment for its maintenance, were often rewarded with recitals or plays at the orphanage and then afterwards sipped fruit juice from paper cups and daintily accepted a butter cookie or two served by the children. In the Christmas pageants, Joseph was often cast as a shepherd boy or one of the Wise Men and the generous offering of applause had unleashed in him sparks of raw energy that stirred his imagination.

During final bows he had gotten into the habit of scanning the faces of the women in the audience. He had a sense that his mother was not among those whose coat collars were adorned with fur or gold brooches. No, she would be seated somewhere in the back where the light was dimmer, camouflaged in shadows. She would be on a secret pilgrimage, returning to the place where she had left her son, to catch a glimpse of him. And Joseph would know her because he was certain that some cosmic current, more intense than darkness, longer than miles of road and years of separation, connected a mother and her child.

It wasn't until Joseph was fourteen, when he was chosen for the finale in a series of vignettes commemorating Lincoln's birthday, that he'd unwittingly been carving for himself a possible route to approval and acceptance. He was to take center stage alone and pay tribute to the soldiers killed at Gettysburg. At first, he approached the performance as nothing more than a recitation of a famous speech. He'd memorize it, deliver it to a politely attentive audience whose collective mind would probably be racing ahead to the conclusion of yet another charitable afternoon when they could return to living their lives in large homes behind finely trimmed privet hedges and in yards of manicured lawns that looked more like green velvet carpeting.

At fourteen, Joseph had grown too tall for the white-gloved hands that patted the heads of the littler waifs. And he was glad of it. For his part he enjoyed the pageants and plays but by then had developed a benign resentment at being paraded on stage with the other children three or four times a year as a way to engender quiet sympathy and a heftier donation. Of course, he knew the money was needed but he could do without the sympathy offered in a certain look or pat on the shoulder. On his own he decided to try and give them a reason to keep coming back, not out of pity or social responsibility but to be truly entertained.

The idea was raw, rootless, lacking clear definition. He knew only that it had to begin with him, inside him, on some level he knew almost nothing about. First, he tried to think of ways he could feel like Lincoln and finally decided it would help if he could dress in something other than his own secondhand white shirt and faded brown corduroys. He wanted a *costume*. Actors wore *costumes*, even if they were ordinary street clothes or dress clothes, they were *costumes*. He sought a certain appearance, one that would lend itself to the reality of Mr. Lincoln. He pored through some old history books, reading all he could to try and develop an impression of what the man might have been like, not what he *looked* like, but what he might have been like in his own time and surroundings. The more he read, the more he wished he possessed some magical power that would allow him to go back to any time in history, walk the streets of another era, talk to the people or just watch and listen. It was a favorite daydream. He pointed to pictures and hounded Lee to please find him the proper clothing. "Please?"

Lee balked, asking the reason for going to so much trouble. "All you got to do is what you done maybe a hundred times before. Just read out some words and smile. When they clap, you is done, take a bow, and that be the end of it. Now, what's all this sudden fuss and bother about, you mind tellin' me?"

Joseph was at a loss to explain what he himself didn't fully understand. "Please?"

And the next afternoon, old Lee took himself down into the dingy cellar and then up into the dusty attic, pushing away cobwebs, searching until he found what he hoped would pass as a bloody costume. "I am cursed with a soft heart," he muttered, handing over a battered top hat and a baggy, black, musty-smelling suit. "And a little luck, huh?"

Joseph was pleased. The clothes would do just fine once they were washed and aired out.

The speech was memorized but something was still wrong. Even with his costume he still didn't feel the part. Whatever he was reaching for was just out of his grasp, right up until the moment he took his place on stage, folded his fingers under the lapels of his coat, and paused. During that brief pause he found a way to feel more like the character he was portraying. The idea came so suddenly that he could almost hear an audible *click* in his brain. He stared out at the audience that was no longer an audience but relatives and friends of the dead soldiers in whose memory they'd gathered and in whose honor their President would now dedicate a memorial.

And then it felt right.

Behind him, the children's chorus set the mood by humming the "Battle Hymn of the Republic." He waited a beat then stepped forward and began.

"Four score and seven years ago our fathers brought forth, on this continent, a new nation, conceived in liberty and dedicated to the proposition that all men are created equal."

He continued with an earnestness he didn't even recognize as belonging to him. He emptied his heart, embracing words that inspired beauty and attention: *dedicate, consecrate, these honored dead....* Joseph paused, stepped left, lifted his chin. He was trying to move as a man of dignity, think as a leader might in that moment, a Commander-In-Chief paying homage to his brave fallen soldiers.

"...these dead shall not have died in vain—that this nation, under God, shall have a new birth of freedom—and that government of the people, by the people and for the people, shall not perish from the earth."

He pulled in a deep breath and exhaled slowly. He had finished without faltering and now stood still, waiting for the applause he'd come to love and appreciate. Waiting...waiting, frozen in place, inside the silence, mouth and lips going dry, hearing murmurs. He quickly surmised he'd made a complete fool of himself, and the audience was stifling their mockery. Sweat beaded on his forehead and the back of his neck was damp. He'd flopped. Perhaps he'd been too theatrical in his performance, too affected. Who did he think he was, Barrymore? If they broke into laughter, he would bolt from the stage...if he could loosen his body out of the terror. He'd run and keep on running until he was far away from Stone Hill. He wanted to run, he did. He stole a sideways glance backstage and saw tears glistening on Lee's dark, wrinkled cheeks. Those few unsettling seconds seemed like long minutes. A man stood up in the back and Joseph thought now they would all start leaving. But then the applause came; slowly at first, rippling over the proscenium, then full blown and sustained. His breath came back normal, his body relaxed. *Okay*, he thought, *it was okay*. He removed his hat, held it by his side, crimping the brim and pressing it to his thigh. He bowed deeply, accepting their praise, then stood tall and straight and felt pride as he smiled back at his audience.

Lee tugged on the stubborn cord, jerking the heavy old curtain closed. He placed a firm hand on Joseph's shoulder as he walked by. "Good work, son," Lee said, the words almost whispered and catching in his throat. "Mighty good."

Joseph hung back for a moment, silent. Tears pinched his eyes at the word *son* and at the sudden realization that for the first time, he had forgotten to look for his mother in the audience. He ran off, folding himself down into an isolated corner where, after his weeping subsided into quiet resignation, he decided she was not there, never had been, and likely never would be. It was time to lay his childish fantasy aside. He wiped at his eyes with his coat sleeves.

"Mama," he whispered, then again, and then once more for the very last time.

About the author:

Lenora Salvucci has been writing stories since her grammar school days and recently has tried her hand at playwrighting as well. The desire to create characters and imagine them in difference situations has never left her.

Her stories have appeared in small magazines and have taken top prizes in local Arts Festivals.

She is also an actress and member of the Actors Studio in Newburyport which is a very active creative arts community. She was born and raised in Lawrence Massachusetts and currently lives in Amesbury MA.

She is very happy to have had her story chosen for publication.

THIS COURSE OF EMPIRE
©2025 by Tim Pingelton

Where are we now? Maybe 300 nautical miles west of the Azores, over 750 nautical miles west of Portugal and far from sight of any land. Over four thousand meters below our daisy petal bobbing on the surface, and under yet another three meters of decomposing skeletons of marine life and rocky sediments, rest the near-petrified hulls of Portuguese cargo vessels. Among the shattered crates that held oranges and imploded casks of port wine lies the remains of Prince Henry the Navigator's exploration crew, who perished on the return voyage after securing a more efficient route by which to ferry slaves to Europe, held down in silence by thousands of tons of pressure.

The surface temperature of this part of the North Atlantic is twenty-one degrees Celsius at noon and twelve by nightfall, but that figure drops four degrees for every ten meters of ocean depth until a terminal temperature of—three degrees is reached. On the oceanic floor of this abyssal desert, the pressure is over sixty kilograms per square centimeter—enough to implode an oxygen tank.

Seawater at this depth could be said to take on properties unlike seawater at Brighton or Torquay. Only fishes with a thick exoskeleton can live in the depths of our setting. There is neither sound nor light.

The eternal Northern Equatorial Current carries Mrs. Thomas Merriweather farther north. Four millimeters of polyvinyl separate her from the blood of the earth. Her valiant husband ran with the yellow plastic cube, which could have fit into a child's lunch box, to the deck where his unconscious bride lay. A yank on the cord filled the rubber raft's sides with smoky air, and he laid her in the center, lifting a shot of her auburn hair from off her eyelids, before he was overtaken by fiery petrol. His navy-blue woolen suit encased him in a thick fire blanket. His captain's bars—awarded for his role in enthusiastically establishing colonization at dear cost to the native population—melted in seconds.

Or maybe we are in a more southerly sea, over the Eltanin Fracture Zone in the South Pacific. Here, some thirty degrees north of the Antarctic Circle, everywhere is nowhere; Land's End ended thousands of nautical miles ago. The tremendous oil fire on the steamer en route to the Cook Islands (call her the *H.M.S. Victoria*, or the *U.S.S. Adams*, or the *Festival Cruiser*) began in Engineering days after losing sight of New Zealand's east shore.

The water here is much like that off the Azores, except colder, deeper, and even more desolate. Desolation, by definition, does have an endpoint, after which there cannot be further desolation. But adrift in this misnomer of an ocean makes one question that restriction. Birds do not inhabit this part of the globe because there is nothing stable on which to alight. Resting on the surface of the water, the species long ago learned, leaves one an easy target for any of the numerous sea creatures frantic for anything with blood.

Regardless of exact geographic location, Mrs. Merriweather, now a widow, awakes with a headache. It is probably sometime in the afternoon; her Cartier Tank wristwatch broke off as she fell into the raft. No human will ever hear its tick again. The airtight plastic raft has made her back sweat profusely, and her smart tweed outfit (tailoring by Abelman) is stained with oil and smudged with soot. The sky is not blue, but a bright grey—maybe the color her husband's hair would have been when he received his first pension check from the service.

She takes off her Donegal jacket gingerly, aware of her precarious situation on that little raft. Her situation is precarious, indeed. Like a ladybug resting on a daisy petal in an eager stream, only the cohesive properties of water keep her atop the flimsy craft. Her hips are below the plane of the oceanic surface, and her silken-clad upper body might now be a canvas sail.

There is no tiller though, leaving her skittering with the whim of the currents flowing pole-ward.

The slight breeze on her rosy cheek is familiar to her, but here there is no thatch cottage on what used to be the outskirts of town; there are no green fields sectioned by stone fences; and there are no mountains denoting the border. The closest mountain to Mrs. Thomas Merriweather is four thousand meters directly below her, past fathom after fathom of ever darkening shades of blue and green and black.

Mrs. Merriweather's blood is over forty degrees centigrade warmer than the water that now teases and toys with the raft. That blood constitutes seventy-one percent of her, and that same percentage of the earth's surface is covered by this non-potable water. Nearly all elements are found in sea water, and all the modern phyla of animals can be found here. It is a life-giving and -sustaining substance that she knows would cause her death if ingested.

As her husband did, she moves her thick hair from her face and is able to see the curvature of the earth, but no evidence of human existence. She notices nothing save her sorry self in the raft and drops her head. Her silks are terribly ripped, and the short heel of her right shoe is broken, revealing the shoemaker's small, sharp brad. She has no left shoe but does not move. The stylized construction of the thistle brooch on her blouse only serves to make her situation all the more desperate, and she carefully unclasps it and drops it into the water. It lazily makes a terminal descent to the ocean floor, glints from the jewels becoming less profuse but more dramatic as it sinks. All is very quiet.

Mrs. Merriweather's brown eyes were not the last to see that finery of bejeweled silver before it settled on the sandy ocean floor.

The cricket ball-sized eye of an *orcas orca* watched the lilting descent. Or should we make it *Monodon monoceros*? Both the killer whale and the narwhal could have witnessed that unique event. They could have noticed this aberrance to normal sea material after ripping apart a huge squid or even one of their own. They fear no predators and consider any creature in their oceans game.

The saddened Mrs. Merriweather sits with her pale legs together and to one side on her little raft, as unknowing as ignorant yet beautiful fowl in a treetop aerie are to a pacing fox below. These maritime foxes, however, weigh over one hundred tons and are deft at scaling trees.

Mrs. Merriweather's forehead is furrowed as she attempts to find the logic in the ivory wedding, the streamer-laden *bon voyage*, the anxiety of honeymoon sex with a man whose rough hand has not even touched her virginal breast. Her quaking sobs cause the sea surrounding her to splash against the raft. She sobs louder, cries. She is screaming sadness, anger, and fear. There is no echo.

She will have no sleep tonight, for the marine air will tighten with hard chill and the strange luminescence of plankton will paint ghostly, painful scenes. The whale sleeps with over one ton of various sea creatures in his cold, cavernous belly. He sleeps near the surface, the distant moon distinguishing his grey or black mottled back from the monotonous colors of the ocean. His misty exhalations of carbon dioxide every twenty minutes or so go unheard by our forlorn castaway; her sensitive ears perceive the sound, but her mind amplifies every sound and creates terrible sounds, so the quiet night is a cacophony of terror.

Starvation and dehydration teamed with hypothermia could send Mrs. Merriweather into a terminal sleep, a minor storm could capsize her tiny vessel, or an unfriendly shark could swallow her and her raft whole. But such is not the case. She drifts two days more. Out of boredom, self-pity, and thirst, she shifts onto her stomach and rests her thin chin on the side of the craft. Looking into the water she is unable to see the cold rocks on the ocean floor, over two kilometers below; she cannot see the creatures whose maritime discoverers thought them to be the spawn of Satan due to their sinister, toothy, demonic appearance. Her pale face matches the bones of Prince Henry, who initiated this course of empire. It matches the flesh of the octopus below, engaged in a morbid battle with a manic barracuda.

Mrs. Merriweather's elegant nose breaks the surface of the water, and her face follows to her ears. She now shares space with such surface creatures as schooling anchovies, jellyfish, and billions of plankton. She opens her eyes and feels no sting, as the pH of sea water matches that of the tears which escaped her depleted lachrymal glands. A flying fish may sail over the raft, but she would not see that either as her eyes are shut again and she is realizing the sensation of the water moving in her slightly bobbing ears.

The motion nearly causes her to fall asleep, but she knows that she, like the carnivorous whales, requires air to breathe. But why does she need it now? One lungful of brine would end it. Or maybe two, she could force herself to take in two.

She opens her eyes again, still submerged, and sees only white. A pink-white. Then something bumps her ear, sounding thunderous in the oceanic silence. She attempts to get her top half back in the raft, but everything is slippery, and she is weak. Her hair is thrown onto her back. Her nose is now one inch from the bulbous head of a Portuguese man-of-war. Her hand pushes it away, causing her to lose balance and drop her head and one shoulder into the water. Her face is wrapped in living gel and then is sharply afire as she struggles back onto the craft.

She is lying on her back, seeing only red. The toxic sting of the jellyfish has lashed a pure white mark diagonally across her face, leaving all other parts fiery red. The pain makes Mrs. Merriweather nauseous, and she manages to vomit in the raft, afraid to attract any more pain with bilious bait overboard. Her eyes swell shut immediately, and her heart pounds painfully in her chest. Gasps come fast, wet, and deep. She can feel that her broken right shoe is gone, both of her pretty shoes now gone.

Soon, Mrs. Merriweather notices that familiar external calm of being lost at sea. She can feel that the sun has set. The light pitching is as it was for the last two and one-half days and her thirst seems to have abated. Her vision is gone, but she knows what the horizon looks like: the net of stars above and nothing breaking the surface of the water save for endless jellyfish. The sounds are again amplified, as they have been every sleepless night; the lapping of the waves at her raft sound louder and louder. There is a new sound, though, whispering in between the waves.

She holds her breath to steady her drumming heart. It is a gurgling sound interspersed with light sounds. A boiling sound followed by a wheezing sound. A leaking sound followed by a hissing sound.

About the author:

Tim Pingelton self-published his first novel, *Art Appreciation*, and has two completed novels awaiting traditional publishing. He also wrote two biographies on Ernest Hemingway for Enslow Publishing. He spends as much time as possible in art museums, and Tim and his wife self-published two volumes (so far) of fun art mystery books titled *Letters from Luis* for grade school kids. Tim lives in Columbia, Missouri, and loves downhill skiing (alas, not in Missouri).

BELLA WANTS A BABY
©2025 by Carole Kelly

Ten years had passed since the Zombie revolution, led by Karl and Bella. Humans had been forced to accept that Zombies, created by a cruel Covid 19 variant known as the Z-Virus, were entitled to live alongside them, with all of the same rights and privileges. It was also agreed that Zombies would never eat Human flesh. Zombie slavery was thus abolished, and Zombies were now free to live their best undead lives.

Bella sighed as she completed the final embellishments to yet another frothy wedding dress in a lurid shade of purple. White, being an unbecoming shade to Zombie complexions, was now usually eschewed in favour of vibrant purple or gold.

After the revolution, Zombies had embraced everything that humanity had to offer, including sex and marriage.

Sex between the undead was possible with extreme care, and lots of lubricant. Vigorous love making ran the risk of unfortunate side effects, such as penis erosion, but was generally considered to be worth the risk, and marriage had once again become a popular institution.

Karl and Bella had been one of the first Zombie couples to marry, and her ambitious wedding dress, a princess style in amethyst-watered silk and gold lace, had helped to launch her successful career. They had been deliriously happy together, until the last few months when Bella had begun to realise that something was missing from their lives. She wanted a baby.

Zombies, being undead, can't become pregnant. Karl's sterile sperm could penetrate her infertile eggs as often as they wished, but her uterus would remain barren.

The dead cannot create life.

Knowing all of this didn't stop Bella from trying, just in case. Karl was at first flattered by the sudden increase in her libido, then became worried that he may sustain injuries from their frantic coupling and began to reject her advances. Even Bella's famed seamstress skills couldn't mend everything.

Bella didn't take the rejection well, and their close relationship began to crack. Fearful of losing his soul mate, Karl was prepared to do anything to make his beloved Bella happy.

One evening after a tense, and largely untouched meal of Bella's favourite rat-flavoured chicken skewers, he took her hands and led her to sit on the balcony of their spacious apartment overlooking the peaceful river.

'Tell me what's wrong, my beautiful,' Karl gently requested in his rich, treacly voice that Bella could never resist.

Bella hung her head, 'I know it's crazy, Karl, but I want a baby. I want to be pregnant and give birth to our child.' She began to sob. Karl tenderly wrapped his arms around her, and she inhaled his familiar scent of cinnamon and cedar, with an underlying tang of decay.

'You know I'll do anything for you, but this isn't possible, Bella. We are undead, there's no IVF for Zombies.'

'I don't care, there must be a way, and I will find it!'

Pulling herself out of his arms, Bella stormed off petulantly, aware that she was being unreasonable, but unable to control her broody hormonal urges.

She had no idea how a pregnancy could be possible, but she was determined to try. Surely this was every woman's right. Just because she was a Zombie, it didn't mean that she wouldn't be a wonderful mother. She'd always seen motherhood and family as part of her future, once her career had become established. Becoming a Zombie, and then a revolutionist, had delayed the establishment of her career as a fashion designer, but now she was ready for that next stage of her life.

During the Zombie Revolution, Bella had made many influential Zombie friends, and she'd become particularly close to Dr Frances Stein, who'd run a successful fertility clinic before contracting the Z-Virus. Dr Frances was passionate about women's rights, and Bella was sure she'd have some ideas about how she could achieve her goal.

The next day she contacted the doctor who was delighted to catch up with her. Once they were cosily settled in Dr Frances' rather messy office, Bella tentatively approached the subject.

'Do you suppose there will ever be a way that a Zombie could give birth?'

'Are you thinking about yourself, Bella? You know the undead can't get pregnant.'

'Yes, I know that...it's just that...oh, Frances, I'd do anything to have a baby!'

Dr Frances looked at her intently. 'Look, there may be a way, but you have to understand that we'd be breaking many laws, and it'll be very risky. There is something theoretical that I've been working on for a while, and I think it might work. You could be my guinea pig, but you must keep this confidential.'

'Of course! Whatever you want me to sign, I'll do it, but what about Karl?'

'He can't be part of this, Bella. I know you trust him, but he's too well known. Can you find a way to disappear for about, oh, nine months?'

Bella thought hard. Her pretty face screwed up in concentration as she tried to think of a story that her darling Karl would accept. There was no way she was going to let this opportunity of motherhood pass.

'I could tell him that I had contracted a rare disease that meant I had to be isolated while they found a cure. Karl's not very knowledgeable about medical stuff. I'm sure he'd believe me. Though we'd have to find a way that he could visit me sometimes.'

'Yes, we could probably do that,' Dr Frances replied vaguely as she began to scribble down ideas. Her brilliant, but eccentric mind, was already planning how to set up the experiment. She'd never thought that she'd actually get the chance to perform a trial. With a hastily repressed chuckle of excitement, she ushered Bella out, with promises to be in touch as soon as she'd selected the right donor.

The next few weeks passed with agonising slowness for Bella. Every day she checked in with Dr Frances in the hope that she was ready to begin but was told to be patient and wait. Lately, the doctor had become irritated by her constant badgering and had told her to stop contacting her. It would happen, but only when everything was in place.

Finally, after what seemed like a lifetime, Bella received the call she'd been waiting for. Tomorrow, she was to check herself into her friend's clinic and be prepared to stay there indefinitely. She needed to tell Karl that she was extremely contagious and that he wouldn't be allowed to visit until she was stable.

Thrilled, Bella packed her bags and made sure she had everything that she needed to maintain her designer business during isolation. Luckily, Karl was away on business for a couple of days, so there were no awkward questions to be answered.

Looking most unlike her usual sleekly groomed self, Dr Frances showed Bella into the room that was going to be her home for the next few months. It was small, with a basic ensuite bathroom and a utilitarian view over the carpark, but had a long workbench for Bella's designs, as she'd requested, and a comfortable armchair.

Bella's bed was surrounded by strange looking monitors and leads that were currently attached to the occupant of the second narrow hospital bed, where a young woman lay unconscious. The slight swell of her stomach suggested the early stages of pregnancy.

Bella turned to Dr Frances in wide-eyed excitement. 'Is that my baby?'

'Hopefully, if all goes well. The implantation will take place today, and after that, you will be tethered to the donor while she nurtures and grows the foetus. This is your last chance, Bella, to change your mind.'

Bella shook her head emphatically. She was single-mindedly focused on this procedure being successful and wasn't going to allow any doubts or guilt to get in the way.

The operation was successful. Bella woke up to find herself linked through multiple leads to the young woman, who was being maintained in an induced coma while her body was being flooded with all the hormones required to fool it into believing that she was still pregnant.

The leads were long enough for Bella to move around the small room, and if necessary, she could easily hide them under a roomy gown, so that Karl couldn't see them when he visited. So far, she felt physically fine, other than some pain from the implantation.

Guiltily, Bella carefully avoided looking at her donor. Dr Frances had assured her that the woman had agreed to the procedure, in exchange for the large sum of money that had been paid over, but Bella wasn't sure that her eccentric friend was telling the truth. However, it was easier on her conscience to just accept the story. Giving birth was all that mattered.

She wasn't looking forward to Karl's visit once he returned. She hated lying to him or causing him distress, but if the outcome was successful, then she was certain that he'd forgive her.

In the end, Karl's visit passed without incident. Restricted to viewing Bella though the window, because of the risk of infection, he didn't notice the other woman hidden behind a partition or the multiple leads attached to her body. Distraught, he sought out Dr Frances for more information about the mystery illness, but she was vague about its nature, and just assured Karl that everything would work out fine. Karl was left running his fingers through his hair in frustration—always an unwise action for a Zombie—and planning to get a second opinion.

The latter proved difficult to find. Human doctors had no interest in Zombie illness, and it turned out that there were very few Zombie doctors. Those who had turned were mainly researchers, and they didn't want to interfere by assessing a patient of the well-respected Dr Frances Stein.

Frustrated, Karl was forced to accept that there was nothing he could do, except visit Bella every day. Still confined to the other side of the window, he was reassured to see that she looked healthy, in an undead fashion, although paler than usual. She even seemed to have put on weight, he thought in surprise, but that was probably the stodgy hospital food.

Bella was finding her pregnancy more difficult than she expected. After the first twenty-four hours, she was wracked with almost constant nausea and stomach pain. Pumped full of drugs to stop her uterus rejecting the baby, she spent her days lying in bed and considering baby names. But not once did she ever consider aborting the alien foetus.

Weeks, then months passed. Karl continued to faithfully visit, and Bella's stomach became bigger and more difficult to conceal, even under her tent-like nightdress. The unwitting and increasingly desiccated donor still lay in a deep coma. Occasionally, Bella had a stab of guilt about the young woman and wondered how she'd ended up in this bizarre situation, but most of the time she just focused on her own pregnancy. As time passed, she began to hesitantly believe that it was really going to happen. She was going to become a mother.

Dr Frances, thrilled to observe her experiment was progressing satisfactorily, began to plan for the birth. She'd already warned Bella that a natural birth wouldn't be possible, and a caesarean was booked for thirty-eight weeks.

The day arrived. Nervous but eager to hold her baby in her arms, Bella allowed herself to be prepped for the operation. She'd chosen not to know the sex but was secretly convinced that she was carrying a boy.

Karl had been told to stay away, as Bella was having a new radical treatment that would probably cure her mysterious disease. Terrified of losing his love, he spent the day pacing around their apartment and tearing out his rapidly thinning hair.

As Dr Frances pulled out a healthy screaming baby boy from Bella's lifeless uterus, the donor on the adjoining bed quietly passed away. Unnoticing, Bella reached out for her son and embraced him with joyful tears. He was perfect. He had a thick head of black hair just like her beloved Karl's and misty blue eyes like her own. Dr Frances had gene-matched with precision. Bella was hoping that the donated hormones would also allow her to breastfeed and lifted her son to her breast with anticipation. He latched on immediately, and Bella felt the visceral tug as milk began to flow into his eager mouth. Happy tears rolled down her pale cheeks as she smiled at Dr Frances, who was misty-eyed herself.

The experiment was deemed to be a great success.

When Karl arrived the next day, chewing his nails in anxiety, he was greeted by a relaxed and smiling Dr Frances who advised him that Bella was well, and that he could finally go in to see her. Oh, and by the way, she had a surprise for him.

Karl rushed into the room from which he'd been banned for nearly nine months. His gorgeous Bella was sitting up in bed, wearing a silky purple nightgown with gold buttons down the front. She was smiling tentatively and holding a bundle of blankets in her arms. Ignoring everything except his beloved Bella, Karl tried to take her in his arms, but the fluffy bundle was in the way.

Bella held up one hand to stop him. 'Karl, I want you to meet your son.'

'What! That's impossible, you can't have a baby.'

'Well, I did! Here he is and he looks just like you.'

Bella tenderly unwrapped the blankets and revealed a sleepy-eyed baby who regarded his adoptive father with disinterest. Karl gently touched his petal-soft cheek, gazing at Bella in shock. Passing the baby to a doting Dr Frances, Bella pulled Karl onto the bed next to her and began to share the story. It took a long time, and by the end, Karl was unsure if he was more horrified by it or just relieved that Bella was okay. The death of the donor worried him, especially as neither of the two women appeared to be concerned. Their focus was entirely on the baby, who was apparently a normal, healthy human boy.

But Karl's concerns were quickly suppressed when he saw how happy Bella was in her newly created motherhood. Her eyes held a sparkle that he realised had been missing for some time.

Dr Frances was able to confidently discharge her patients after three days. Karl had hastily set up a nursery for baby James, named after his father, and watched as Bella lovingly tucked him into his bassinet. Afterwards, she lay with Karl on their bed and snuggled into his arms. Breathing in her familiar scent of overripe plums and burnt sugar, now tainted with a whiff of sour milk, he began to relax. Now that Bella had her baby, everything would be okay.

Baby James grew quickly and soon began to demand more solid food than Bella's breast milk. Secretly relieved, as he was constantly drawing blood with his sharp little milk teeth every time he fed, Bella introduced him to a variety of approved baby foods. James proved to be very particular in his tastes, scorning the bland vegetable mushes and demanding meat-based meals. By the time he was six months old, he was able to suck and chew a piece of rare steak with great enthusiasm. Bella thought he was cute, but Karl found his adopted son unnerving and unnatural. He'd failed to develop any bond with him, and James appeared to be aware of his feelings as he refused to let Karl hold him. This was causing problems, especially as Bella had hoped to begin spending more time in her business. She had a backlog of needy brides waiting for their purple designer wedding dresses.

Karl suggested a nanny to help out. At first, they tried Zombie nannies, but James refused to accept them as mother substitutes and screamed so loudly that the women left in disgust. At last, a sweet young human girl applied for the position. She wasn't very experienced, but James took to her immediately, and Bella felt confident to leave her precious son in her care while she spent some time in her studio.

For the first few weeks everything went well. James appeared to be content, and Bella was able to juggle motherhood and career with some confidence. Karl, relieved to have more alone time with his beloved Bella, began to hope that their relationship could regain its former closeness, which had been damaged since the unexpected arrival of a baby.

One afternoon, Karl arrived home earlier than usual. His high-ranking position in local government meant that he often worked long hours, but today he'd planned to finish early so that he could surprise Bella with a special meal to celebrate their anniversary. When he entered the apartment, it was quiet, and he assumed that nanny Jessica had taken James to the park. Wrinkling his nose at the metallic smell of blood, he made a mental note to tell the girl to clean up better after James's meals. He opened the kitchen windows to let in some clean air. Dumping the shopping on the table, he wandered into the bedroom to change into something more comfortable. The smell was stronger here and Karl began to worry. The nursery adjoining their luxurious bedroom appeared to be the source of the overwhelming odour.

Karl braced himself, he may be a revolutionist, but he had a phobia about blood. However, Bella would never forgive him if something had happened to her precious baby. Reluctantly entering the nursery, Karl's first sight was of James contentedly playing with his blocks. Karl relaxed his tense shoulders, then noticed the blood stains on the fluffy white rug. Where was the nanny? She shouldn't have left James alone.

He looked around the cheerfully painted room. The sunny yellow walls were now carmine splashed, and there were signs of a desperate struggle. James's collection of teddies was also blood-splattered, and the smell of offal was turning Karl's delicate stomach. He moved towards James, intending to pick him up and remove him from this chamber of horror, then stopped in shock. The blocks James was stacking were not made from wood but appeared to be well-sucked spinal bones. Looking more closely,

Karl realised in ever increasing horror that James was covered in blood, none of which was his own. He smiled toothily at Karl, revealing pieces of partially chewed intestine looped around his baby teeth.

Trembling with fear and disgust, Karl backed away.

Dr Frances's risky experiment had not been the success she'd hoped for. How was he going to tell Bella that her adored baby was a real Zombie, and that he was going to have to destroy it.

Their marriage would never be the same.

About the author:

Carole lived in NZ and the UK before finally settling in Australia.

Her early careers have included window dressing, debt collection, an allied health practice and working for the British Civil Service. In Australia Carole completed a Master's in Counselling & Applied Psychotherapy and thereafter has specialised in relationship therapy.

Carole has been writing for most of her life but only started to take it seriously in the last few years. Her first published work was 'Cerelia', a dystopian post-holocaust fiction, which is included in the anthology 'The Four Season Project', released in 2022. She has since been published in several other anthologies, including in 2024, 'Spawn 2: More Weird Horror Tales About Pregnancy, Birth and Babies', and 'Monsterthology 3'.

ARTHUR SMYTHE AND ME
©2025 by Emely Bennett

Part One

Arthur Smythe had disappeared. One Friday afternoon, he left the bank where he worked—and never returned.

Weeks later, a group of his co-workers met after work at their local pub to discuss Arthur's unexplained disappearance. Upper management had no information, or that's what they wanted everyone to believe. No one did, though. That's why Luke, from Operations, decided to arrange their get-together.

Arthur Smythe was very reserved, never socializing with other staff members. They tried because they considered themselves a friendly group, but Arthur, always polite, kept to himself. Alexander, from Human Resources shared that Arthur had been brought in to do some in-depth, "hush-hush" banking research.

They estimated he was in his late thirties or early forties, over six feet tall, medium build, always impeccably dressed, sporting a neatly trimmed beard, perfectly parted brown hair, and dark eyes that peered through black horn-rimmed glasses.

Arriving at the bank every morning at precisely 8:30, he would hang his suit coat on the hook in his office, sit down, and take some papers out of his briefcase. Everyone surmised it was extra work he had taken home the day before.

He'd leave his office unerringly at 10 a.m. to brew his own coffee in the small employee kitchenette, using his own special blend. At exactly 12:15 p.m. he'd take a lunch bag out of his briefcase, put on his coat if necessary, and go outside to sit in the park beside the bank building to enjoy his lunch. In inclement weather, he would go to the little café across the street from the bank, sit at the back corner table, order something to drink with his lunch, and read some kind of financial publication. At 1:30 he'd be back at his desk working until 3:30 at which time he'd leave his office, go to the kitchenette, brew another coffee, and return to his desk. At precisely 5:15 he'd gather the papers to put into his briefcase, clear his desk, put on his coat, and leave the building.

Betty, the receptionist, said, "As you know, I stay until 5:45 p.m. and when he passed by, I'd always say, 'See you tomorrow, Mr. Smythe.' He'd nod and smile. He did the same thing on that last Friday when I said, 'See you Monday, Mr. Smythe.' He never gave any indication that he wasn't planning on returning."

Mabel, from Customer Relations, continued. "I never actually spoke to him but, Alice, who couldn't be here, told me she had tried to start a conversation with him several times but never succeeded, and everyone knows that if anyone can get someone to talk about themselves, it's Alice."

"You could set your watch by his movements, and it would always show the correct time. Wasn't that right, Norman?" Luke asked.

Norman, whose office was next to Arthur's, replied, "Right. It was strange, though: that last Friday he worked, he left at 3:15—quite a bit earlier than usual."

"That's right," Betty exclaimed. "He did leave early that Friday. Definitely unusual!"

Everyone agreed that break in his strict schedule was indeed puzzling, and wondered if Arthur's exit from his day-to-day office routine may have had something to do with that anomaly. They concluded that they would never really know what happened and should let the matter drop. None of them could, though. If someone at the bank inadvertently mentioned his name, his unexplained disappearance would again become the topic of their conversations over the next few days.

There it is, readers—Part One of our new four-part story. Exactly what had happened to Mr. Arthur Smythe? Be sure to check back in our next edition and maybe you'll find out!

*****

"And there it is, readers," I said aloud, imitating the voice of a popular talk show host. I closed my laptop, having finished reading—again—Part One of my story. Seeing it on a popular, biweekly magazine's website was so exhilarating!

I live alone so I'm my own audience. I'm not at the point where I'm starting to answer myself so that's a plus, I guess.

Yawning and stretching I realized it was almost 11:30 p.m. and I had just enough time to freshen up a bit before leaving for work. Hopefully it's a busy night tonight or I may fall asleep.

I host a midnight to 5 a.m. show four nights a week (Wednesday being my night off) at our local radio station taking call-in requests while tapping my feet to Country and Western music. Yes, there are those who still listen to the radio at midnight. It still surprises me just how many people are awake in those early morning hours.

I'm also a freelance writer, not that it pays that well, but writing is my passion, and I get by. I'm now at that age where I'm looking for something more secure. I'm in my mid-twenties—okay, early thirties—single, with a social life that's been non-existent for quite a while. I'm also tired of working midnights and have to start seriously thinking about how to fund a comfortable retirement one day. That's why it was so exciting to land this opportunity—it's actually an eight-week "probational opportunity"—with this popular, highly rated online magazine. Hopefully, it works out.

I'm an avid people-watcher and in doing so will sometimes get a story idea which I immediately jot down in my ever-present notebook. *For instance, last week I was enjoying dinner with a friend at our favourite pub before I started my shift. The group sitting at the next table weren't being very quiet—they were discussing a co-worker who had simply left his job and disappeared without so much as a goodbye. I thought there may be a story there. Another idea came one Wednesday when I decided to get up early, grab something from the nearby diner and enjoy my lunch in our neighbourhood park.*

Sitting on a park bench, munching away, I noticed an average-looking guy sitting on the bench across from mine having his lunch while reading a book. A pretty, thirty-something woman (who seemed to be having a problem balancing her large, cumbersome shoulder-strap purse, along with another heavy bag, plus her coffee) walked by his bench and suddenly stumbled. She held on to her coffee but not her bags. I immediately jumped up to help but he was faster. Soon they were sitting together enjoying their coffees while having, I imagined, one of those get-to-know-you conversations.

That got me thinking. Was that stumble real or contrived? Were either of them actually who they appeared to be, or were they each living a secret life?

Enter Arthur, and a thirty-something female named Annie...

ARTHUR SMYTHE AND ME
Part Two

My name is Annie O'Brien and I'm currently under contract with a private investigative firm that shall remain nameless, owned by Mr. X, who has another name, too, but I don't know it and I'm okay with that.

I was contacted through various faceless channels by his intermediary, who unsurprisingly called herself Ms. Y. I was told that Mr. X is very well known, very rich, and prefers to stay anonymous. I don't care. I only need to know the few necessary facts to do my job. Any other information is superfluous and not worth my time.

Apparently, Arthur Smythe, a financial wizard, recently held a high executive position with Mr. Z (of course), a business associate and close friend of Mr. X. According to Ms. Y, a large amount of money was not where it was supposed to be—an extremely large amount of money that wasn't reported on their corporate income tax return. I don't know exactly how much because it's irrelevant. Apparently, Arthur had given his notice rather suddenly and then simply disappeared just days before Mr. Z discovered that funds in an offshore account had vanished. Coincidence? Maybe. Mr. Z didn't think so. Tracking him down using conventional means was unsuccessful; thus, the need for my services.

I don't advertise but word gets around in certain circles and every once in a while I'm approached, usually through an intermediary, like Ms. Y, to do a highly confidential job. If the job doesn't interest me, I turn it down. Even if it does, it depends on my schedule. I've been doing this for years now so my track record would speak for itself if I ever chose to divulge it. Which I won't. I'm very expensive but I'm also the best. Like that saying goes, "you get what you pay for". To my knowledge, there's never been any complaints and, believe me, I make it my business to know.

I have my own ways of finding helpful information—sometimes legal, sometimes not. Okay, most of the time...not. I've never had to use force because I'm strictly non-violent. I could, though, but only if it was absolutely necessary and I had no other choice. In those extremely rare instances, just showing pictures of some well-muscled acquaintances and threatening to send one of them for a visit usually does the trick.

As well as tracking down missing individuals when I feel like it, I have my own personal pastime enjoying and utilizing my, shall I say, exceptional procurement skills. An incredible amount of research and planning on my part is imperative, especially if it involves a bit of danger (which I love), and it usually does. Simply put, I relieve certain organizations, individuals, and even museums of their *objets d'art*—it's a profitable market especially with various international private collectors who are a bit unscrupulous and willing to pay what it takes to get what they want. I'm always successful but also extremely cautious. I complete a job then lie low—sometimes up to a year if necessary. I don't want to be on any agency's radar. It's been working quite well; however, in the very unlikely event that I should have to disappear quickly, I'm prepared with a safety deposit box holding everything I require. In my business, one can't be too careful.

I don't need the extra income thanks to an inheritance from a loving grandmother that was invested very wisely. I do it because— well, because I can. Grandmother also left me her special tool that she felt no woman should be without. Apparently, it had come in very handy a couple of times during her lifetime. I haven't had to use it yet, but it's always with me—just in case.

Getting back to Arthur Smythe. After completing my usual due diligence, I was satisfied that Ms. Y was legit, so I assumed Messrs. X and Z would be as well. It was a chance I wouldn't normally take, but I was in one of my lying low periods and felt this would relieve some of the restlessness and boredom I sometimes felt during my latest hiatus. I took the job just to pass some time although this search didn't sound all that difficult. I had been forewarned by Ms. Y that Arthur was extremely intelligent, but that's not a problem. The same has been said about me.

In her latest communication, Ms. Y indicated that Mr. Z was becoming agitated. "Sweating bullets" were her exact words. I advised her that I had clearly stated at the onset of our relationship that finding Arthur would "take as long as it takes". I could continue or not. His choice. I really didn't care. I did mention, however, that if Arthur was not found, Mr. Z could certainly be facing some very dire, legal consequences.

As I expected, Mr. Z made an intelligent decision. I continued with the search.

Of course, I found Arthur—despite the fact that he must have had outside help with his vanishing act because no one could disappear like he did without it. It took seven days. Surprisingly, I enjoyed every minute of this particular assignment as it was just what I needed. I should have informed Ms. Y weeks ago that I had found their elusive missing person, and picked up my fee, but I didn't. I decided to stay and perhaps get to know Arthur on a more, shall we say, personal level. He appealed to me, and I wanted to understand why.

Because of that decision, there are now a couple of problems. Big problems. Unexpectedly, and totally out of character, I'm starting to have feelings for this man, which isn't smart, not smart at all. Also, I have a suspicion that Arthur is beginning to sense that I'm not who I'm supposed to be. It's just one of those uneasy thoughts right now, but it's there. If I'm right, though, there may be unpleasant consequences—for both of us. I hope I'm wrong.

So, readers—what do you think? Why does Annie feel uneasy about Arthur? Check out our next edition for Part Three!

*****

I should explain the magazine's "probational opportunity" for writers. It's very unconventional—a continuing story appearing in four issues over eight weeks. The story's conclusion will be followed by an online ratings chart for readers to submit along with their comments. Based on the final ratings score and readers' feedback, the magazine's editor will decide whether or not I passed the probationary period.

It's a little unusual. Well, a lot unusual and a bit weird, but if it means a permanent position with this successful magazine (including benefits and a pension plan), I can do unusual and weird.

ARTHUR SMYTHE AND ME
Part Three

Once I discovered Arthur's whereabouts, I decided to find a job close to the bank where he worked—much easier to track his movements that way. I was lucky and found one as a server in the little café almost across the street from the bank. Perfect. Serving is one of my favourite undercover jobs and I'm very good at it. Most people, except for the odd one, are friendly and always ready to chat. It's amazing how much information one can learn while serving talkative customers.

It didn't take long to determine Arthur's lunch time routine. In good weather, he would go to the nearby park, sit on the same park bench and enjoy his lunch; if it wasn't, he'd come into the café, sit at the back corner table by the window, and order something to drink, having brought in his own prepared lunch. He always had some sort of reading material with him—usually financial in nature. I decided it would be best to approach him outdoors as I didn't want to attract anyone's notice inside the café.

Our meeting wasn't, I'm almost embarrassed to say, very original. I could have taken longer to come up with a better plan, but I didn't want to wait—it was time to make the initial contact. I timed my own lunch break while he was having his in the park. Carrying a large, unwieldy shoulder-strap purse, a bulky bag containing various items (the bag needed to appear somewhat heavy and awkward), and a large coffee, I strolled leisurely past his bench when I suddenly stumbled. I managed to hold on to my coffee, dropping my bag while letting my purse slide off my shoulder. Not very creative but it worked. Arthur was up like a flash, offering his help, and soon I was sitting comfortably beside him on the park bench enjoying my coffee, and having a short, let-me-introduce-myself conversation.

He seemed quite reserved and would definitely be a challenge, but I thrive on challenges. I reported back to Ms. Y that I had made considerable progress and should be successful within the next few weeks—that should satisfy Messrs. X and Z, and it did.

I left it for a couple of days and then accidentally bumped into Arthur again at the park where I supposedly went to read a book during my lunch break. He looked surprised—happy surprised, actually—and asked me to join him. He was quite nice, and we had a very interesting conversation. I mentioned that I had always wanted a degree in Economics (a subject we would have in common) and, after a small inheritance, was able to attend part-time university classes besides working at the café. He seemed very interested, and our conversation continued smoothly.

Staying away for a few more days, I returned to the park and was gratified to see a crooked grin when he saw me approaching. I told him that unfortunately my lunch break time had changed which meant I'd be on a different schedule than his. I was somewhat dismayed as he didn't show the reaction I was expecting and wondered if I was losing my touch. Four days later he was sitting in my section of the café even though it was a beautiful sunny day outside. I hadn't lost my touch after all. This was proving to be a rather interesting assignment.

Lunches became dinners followed by evenings in his apartment, discussing whatever happened to be newsworthy that week. He was very well-read, and our time together was thought-provoking and quite enjoyable. My feelings for Arthur were changing, and I knew I was entering dangerous territory.

One night we had a lively discussion about the machinations of the financial world and why some people take such enormous stock market risks, and recently he spoke about the sometimes dark, secretive world of art and art collectors. I didn't contribute much to this conversation, just making short comments every so often. I listened intently, though, as he made some very interesting points. The discussion seemed a little too close for comfort. Could he link an Economics student/café server to an art thief? Hopefully not, but I still felt a little uneasy.

Last night, while enjoying our after-dinner liqueur, Arthur took my hand.

"Annie, would you like to go away with me? An opportunity came up for one of the bank's senior executives. He wasn't available so he's offered it to me. A weekend in a beautiful house surrounded by white beaches on a private island just off the coast. I could leave the bank earlier on Friday so that we can drive into the city, stay overnight at that luxurious downtown hotel, and travel to the island early Saturday morning."

This was totally unexpected. I was slowly making progress but he was still somewhat reserved. I thought it would take me at least a couple more weeks to get this far in our relationship.

Not wanting to appear too eager, I hesitated for a few moments before answering, "Let me think about it and I'll let you know tomorrow. Is that okay?"

"Of course. I know it's a bit sudden but I didn't want to refuse. Oh, by the way," he added, "I'll take care of all the expenditures. I just want you to enjoy yourself."

Expenditures? Who says that? Only a financial expert, I suppose. I knew Arthur could afford it. At my first opportunity, I'd taken the liberty to quickly rifle through his briefcase which he had inadvertently forgotten to lock. Stupid mistake on his part. I found some interesting bank statements tucked away deep inside one of the pockets—three statements from three different offshore accounts. No wonder Mr. Z was sweating bullets.

I didn't sleep well. Was I taking too much of a risk trusting Arthur despite some unease that's never gone away?

"So?" Arthur asked a bit anxiously while having lunch at the café the following day.

"The trip sounds wonderful," I replied nonchalantly, "but I have an assignment due at the end of next week, so I had to decide—a weekend away or Economics?"

"And?"

"I'd rather spend the time in a beautiful island house where there's lots of sun and white beaches—with you, of course." I replied with a smile.

"I'll make the arrangements as soon as I get back to the bank," Arthur replied with that crooked grin of his that was becoming so endearing.

That's how we ended up enjoying a delicious dinner on Friday night in the posh dining room of that downtown hotel, savouring an Irish Coffee as the perfect ending before we went back to Arthur's suite. A suite, of all things.

Standing in the hallway, outside his door, he turned to me, grinned, and then instead of inserting his key card, knocked. Strange.

"I've arranged a little surprise for you."

So, readers—what's Arthur's little surprise? Should Annie trust him? Find out in two weeks while reading the conclusion of this story!

*****

The conclusion—two conclusions, actually—one to my story, and one to my probationary opportunity. Will I score high on the ratings chart? Will I finally have a permanent job with benefits and a pension plan? It's very nerve-wracking, and now I'm the one sweating bullets!

ARTHUR SMYTHE AND ME
Conclusion

A little surprise? My radar immediately shot up. A well-dressed, older lady opened the door.

"There you are! Come on in, we've been waiting for you."

Two businessmen sitting on the couch, enjoying a drink, immediately stopped talking as soon as we walked in.

"Arthur..." I began but he interrupted.

"Annie, meet my colleagues. I believe you know who they are although you haven't formally met. First, let me introduce you to the anonymous Mr. X. X is a high-ranking executive in a very distinguished international banking corporation. Banking has become quite routine for him over the years, so he's found something more exciting to help break the tedium. He's very tech-savvy—expertly assembling, when required, unquestionable background checks, providing authentic-looking bank statements among other financial documents, and arranging fictional 'hush-hush' banking jobs courtesy of his trusted, and very well-paid, associates who never ask questions."

Mr. X nodded.

"And Ms. Y, our talented intermediary," Arthur continued.

She at least smiled.

"Y is an international art expert hoping to reward herself with a few pieces of her own. And, of course," he continued, "your employer, Mr. Z, the Senior Investigative Officer in a well-known international criminal investigative firm. Unfortunately, Z never receives the recognition he deserves."

Mr. Z gave me, of all things, a salute.

"X, Y, and Z," I replied sarcastically.

I looked towards Arthur. "You?"

He laughed. The reserved individual I thought I was getting to know over these past weeks instantly disappeared.

"Just call me, Arthur. I'm actually getting used to that name."

There was something else I could call him, and it certainly wasn't

Arthur.

"Imagine," he continued, "four international experts and their meticulous planning have successfully apprehended the notorious art thief who's been on all our most wanted lists for quite a few years."

"And who might that be?" I asked.

"Now, don't be modest," he answered. "After tracking these thefts for quite some time, we finally ascertained that they were actually committed by one person. It took longer than we had anticipated, but worth the effort. You always do such an excellent job covering your tracks and then disappearing. We call you 'The Chameleon' because of your ability to change identities to fit into any job or social circle required. Who would have guessed that a beautiful, petite female was the mastermind behind these incredible robberies, wreaking such havoc on the art world and their insurance companies—neither of which appreciate or admire your exceptional talents?"

"I see," I said, surreptitiously assessing my situation.

"We decided to join forces and establish our own clandestine investigative team," Arthur continued, "'borrowing', of course, the latest technology and information from our different agencies. Z and I have worked together for years and have always been quite successful. Together, we came up with this brilliant plan. And then, as Archimedes once said, 'Eureka!'. Imagine what a coup this would be for all of us if we turned you in," Arthur added, having the audacity to grin that endearing, crooked grin that now looked more like the Joker's sinister grin in the *Batman* movies. Suited him much better.

"We have a proposition for you," X finally spoke.

"We truly admire your work," Y added.

"Join our team," Z continued.

"So, this is your little surprise, Arthur?" I asked, looking directly at him. I was going to knock that smug look off his face one way or another. Feigning a cough, I opened my small clutch purse, supposedly looking for a tissue, and quickly pulled out the "special tool" Grandmother felt no woman should be without—a beautiful, silver derringer.

"Just happen to have a little surprise for you, too," I said pointing it at a lower part of Arthur's body because, being a thief not a killer, I just wanted to inflict some extreme but treatable pain.

I felt a sudden burning in my thigh. I hadn't heard anything, just felt it. I looked over at Y and saw that she was holding a little surprise in her hand, too. Wow, she was quick. That was my last thought before darkness descended.

I opened my eyes. I was lying on a very comfortable bed, feeling light-headed, and extremely thirsty. I wanted water, lots of water.

There was someone else here, sitting in a chair by the window working on a laptop. It wasn't Arthur—no neatly trimmed beard, perfectly parted brown hair, or dark eyes peering through black, horn-rimmed glasses. This guy was clean-shaven, with disheveled, dark blond hair, and eyes that apparently had perfect vision.

He must have sensed something for he looked up. I could see brilliant blue eyes and a familiar, crooked grin. Arthur? No, it couldn't be.

"Water," I croaked.

"Of course," the maybe Arthur answered getting up to fill a water glass for me.

Sitting up and gulping the water I felt much better. I looked at this person more closely. It was Arthur all right.

"You didn't think that I'd end a relationship that was just beginning to get so interesting, did you?"

I didn't answer.

"Are you actually angry with me?"

I stayed silent.

"Want to know where we are?"

I stared at him, wanting to get up to land a punch right on his nose but I didn't have the energy. As soon as I did, though, I would.

"We're in a lovely house, which I own, on a beautiful private island, which I also own, where we had planned to spend the weekend," he continued. "Remember discussing how some people take incredible stock market risks? I didn't mention it at the time, but I did that once, and along with an amazing stroke of luck, became very, very rich. I still work with Z, though, keeps me from getting bored. Apprehending 'The Chameleon'? Couldn't resist it."

I continued to stare at him.

"Annie, hear me out."

"No," I finally responded, "I don't trust you."

Sitting down on the bed, he replied, "I don't trust you either."

Taking something from his pocket, he asked, "Were you actually going to shoot me?" handing me my derringer.

I took it and remained silent.

"X, Y, and Z arrive tomorrow. Y came upon a remarkable opportunity and, after discussing it with me, she's presenting it to everyone tomorrow afternoon. We both decided it was time to reap some paybacks of our own. Interested in joining us?"

I didn't answer.

Smiling that stupid Joker grin, he continued, "Oh come on, Annie, if we move forward with this, we'll need someone like you with very exceptional skills to pull it off."

"Not. Interested."

"You will be once you hear what I have to say. Just listen."

"No."

I did anyway. It sounded intriguing with just the right amount of danger, piquing my interest.

Besides, I *do* have those very exceptional skills.

So, readers, what do you think? We value your opinion so please rate *Arthur Smythe and Me* and submit your comments on the online ratings chart on page 27. Thanks for participating!

*****

It's been almost three years since the success of my "probational opportunity" at the magazine and so much has happened since then.

After reviewing the results and the readers' comments from the online survey, Harry (the magazine's editor) offered me the position and, of course, I immediately and enthusiastically accepted.

According to the online comments, many hoped to read more stories featuring Annie and Arthur. Two additional short stories based on the duo's escapades and their budding love-hate relationship appeared in the magazine, resulting in Annie and Arthur becoming a favourite with the readers.

Much to my surprise, the posted comments caught the attention of Frank, a publishing agent, who requested a meeting. I learned he searched for stories written by emerging authors and believed that Annie and Arthur and their exploits would make a popular book—perhaps even a series. I wasn't so sure but after much thought and advice, I knew it was now or never—I wasn't getting any younger. I decided to work on the book but keep my job with the magazine. After all, I did need to eat and pay my bills. Besides, Harry was there.

What followed were many, many false starts and everything in between, including a number of "What-have-I-done?" and "I-can't-do-this!" tantrums, plus a couple of embarrassing, hysterical episodes in Harry's office. Harry was so supportive, ready to offer help and his shoulder to cry on. How he put up with me I'll never understand. Frank, maintaining complete confidence in my writing, contacted a number of publishers. After reading my manuscript, one of them offered a few recommendations, followed by an actual contract and a small advance! We took it!

Guess where I'm sitting right this minute. I'm at my first book signing, and there's a line of readers waiting for me to sign their copy! Yes, an actual 352-page book (the first in the new Annie and Arthur trilogy) now being promoted online and in bookshops!

I'm still working at the magazine—just can't give it up—and it's not only because of benefits and a pension plan. It's where I met my Harry.

It's hard to believe how much my life has changed—and it all started with a short story....

About the author:

Growing up on a farm in southwestern Ontario, Emely Bennett spent many happy hours with her Grandmother listening to stories of the "olden days" when her grandmother was young. Storytelling became a part of Emely's life, so it wasn't surprising that English Composition remained her favourite class throughout her school years.

Emely retired as Executive Assistant to the Executive Director of a non-profit organization near Toronto, Ontario. Her first short story, "Jimmy's Swing", was one of fifteen entries selected to be included in the Stories through the Ages 2022 anthology.

In addition to keeping tabs on her family who seem to be spread all over the province, Emely keeps quite busy with reading, gardening, volunteering, and working on her next short story.

CLOWNING AROUND
©2025 by Marilee Aufdenkamp

Stanley Nowka had been clowning for two years. Not as a primary means of income, that was second-shift at the assembly station at the Becton Dickinson factory, fitting together syringe barrels and plungers. Clowning for pay was mostly children's birthday parties and a few small corporate gigs. Being a thirty-year-old, never married, late in life only child of two only children, Stanley wasn't all that comfortable around the younger set. Clowning for *pay* he didn't much care for, but he needed the money and, when his mother was alive, he'd gotten a certificate for completing a 10-unit online course from the Los Angeles Clown School. *Volunteer* clowning at the old folks' home was a different story. He liked it a lot.

Stanley peered into the lighted Walmart make-up mirror he'd placed on the makeshift ironing-board-vanity he'd fashioned for himself in his room at the Havana Inn. He had no idea why a small-town motel in the middle of Nebraska would be called the Havana Inn. What was important to him was that it was cheaper than renting a house or an apartment and they let rooms by the night, week, or month.

Even if a freshly shaved face wasn't an absolute necessity before *slapping on the grease paint* as they liked to say in the clown forums, it felt great. He patted his cheeks. No wonder men used to pay for the straight razor and hot towel treatment in the olden days, not that it would have been a luxury he could have afforded. He picked up his small cup of Clown White face paint. Who knew before clown school that there were different types of clowns and that not all clowns were whiteface? Whiteface were the boss clowns. He was definitely not a boss clown. He was an *Auguste* clown, the clumsy, zany, clown with the glued-on nose, oversized shoes, and ill-fitting, mismatched jackets and pants.

"Auguste. It's *Ah* like when the doctor says, 'Open wide' and comes at your throat with the wooden stick, and *goost* like the honking duck-relative, but with a 't' on the end," he liked to say when people mispronounced it like the month following July. "*Auguste* is German slang—or more precisely Berliner slang—for idiot."

He put a dab of Clown White on his left hand at the base of his thumb, reminding himself of the old salt and tequila maneuver usually performed by some wild and carefree character in the movies. Leaving it there for a moment or two helped it warm up, so it was easier to apply. He started by patting the Clown White into his eyebrows to make them disappear. He would draw new ones, slightly higher than his own, that would wiggle and stand out with exaggerated facial movements. He extended the white a little above his natural brow line and carried it down along the outside and slightly under each eye. This was the first step in making his eyes appear as large as possible. A make-up sponge would clean up the lines when he applied the peach-toned base to the rest of his face, before finishing with the embellishments he'd perfected for his clown's mouth. Theatrical powder would set the make-up so that he could rub his eyes, swelter in the sun, or get sprayed with a hose by an out-of-control child—which had actually happened—and everything would stay in place.

"Well, hello, Skippy," the nurse in Pod One called out to him when he entered the building.

Skippy was his clown-name, and also what his grandpa called him when he was a little boy. He'd been coming to Happy Manor since his mother became a resident there the year before her passing, and he'd been clowning there the first Saturday of every month almost ever since.

Lunch was being served in the Central Dining Room where the less frail and more cognitively sound residents ate. There was a small stage there, at the north end, where he performed. He didn't use many props with his senior audience, just the usual juggling balls, a ukelele, disappearing scarves, a magic wand, a large foam hand, and giant playing cards. And this month he'd brought plastic kazoos that he'd found online for the bulk rate price of $34.99 for 104 units—free shipping. Mr. and Mrs. Patel, the accommodating owners and onsite managers of the Havana Inn, allowed the long-termers to use the motel office as a mailing address.

What he really wanted was a unicycle. What a potential blast it would be, riding among the tables in the Central Dining Room. The old folks would love it. Unfortunately, it was all he could manage to cover his own monthly living expenses, and he already had a fair amount invested in clowning. Anyway, Administration would likely worry that he'd bump into someone and knock them down. He had the equipment for balloon animals—he was fairly skilled at wiener dogs and elephants—but he usually reserved the hand pump and balloons for the kids' birthday parties.

One prop he never left behind was the walking stick given to him by the family of Mr. Kaufman, one of the residents, after his passing. It was a fine old walking stick, made of highly polished wood topped with a cheerful carved frog figure with wide eyes, a sheepish grin, and a tiny tilted top hat. The walking stick was a beloved part of his act.

After a rousing rendition of "When the Saints Go Marching In" with Stanley, or Skippy, on the ukelele and forty-four residents on kazoos—easy to calculate since there were eleven tables in the dining room—the crowd cheered. Those who were able stood up and clapped.

"Encore, encore!" some of them yelled, pounding utensils on the tables. Stanley finished with a sweet rendition of "What a Wonderful World", then after a few hello's—he knew most of the residents who came to the Central Dining Room—he pulled a vacated chair to his mother's old table.

"Your momma would have been so proud," Connie said. Connie and his mom had been first-rate Tuesday night Bingo buddies.

Lana, the kindly but quiet food service aide who'd worked at Happy Manor since Stanley had been coming to visit his mom, was busy clearing tables across the room.

Gordon nudged Stanley in his clown-ribs with his elbow. "You ought to ask Lana if she'd like to go out for coffee after work," Gordon said.

Gordon had been Stanley's mom, Janice's, biggest fan. Gordon had finagled a seat at his mom's table after old Mr. Clark had gotten too frail to come to the dining room. Gordon was always interested in relationships, especially romantic ones.

"You couldn't pay me to get involved with a man again at my age," Stanley's mother used to tell Stanley when she'd describe how hard Gordon tried to court her.

"I'm not kidding," Gordon said. "You should have seen old Lana smiling from ear to ear the whole time you were up there clowning."

It was funny to hear old Gordon calling a woman of probably no more than thirty, *old* Lana.

"I've never seen her looking so lively," Gordon said.

Life at Becton Dickinson was uneventful the following week and, before Stanley was ready, it was time for him to clown at little Olivia's eighth birthday party. He parked the car around the corner from his destination. Clowns don't drive seventeen-year-old Toyota Corollas with fading paint, rust spots low on the back panels, and 178,000 miles on the odometer. Clowns drive goofy pedal cars or little motorized go-carts like the ones the Shriners drive in the Amber Huey Parade on Thanksgiving weekend. The party was in progress and, as instructed, he entered the backyard through the side gate.

"A clown!" the kids screamed nearly in unison. They rushed toward him. One little girl cried and ran to her mother.

There, ahead of him, was the concrete slab adjacent to the covered porch where he'd been instructed to set up. The parents sat under the shade of the covered porch, but they wanted him out in the bright sunshine where the children could see him better, little Olivia's mother had explained. The porch eaves cast a few inches of shadow along the edge of his workspace and there he placed his trunk of props in the resultant shade. The kids formed a semi-circle around him.

"Who's the birthday girl?" he called out, marching around in his oversized clown shoes. He pointed to one of the fathers. "Are *you* the birthday girl?" he asked, and the kids roared.

"*I'm* the birthday girl," Olivia said, stepping forward and putting her hands on her hips.

Skippy the Clown scratched his wild orange hair and pretended to think. After a moment or two, he marched over to his trunk with exaggerated steps and brought back a shiny, black, top hat and wand. He put the hat on, took it off, turned it over and over appearing to inspect it, waved the magic wand over it, then reached in and pulled out a stuffed Dalmatian. Olivia's favorite, her mother had told him when they were on the phone finalizing details. He stood directly in front of Olivia, bent deeply at the waist and, in a grand gesture, presented her with the red-collared plush canine.

"Oh, let me see," a little girl in a unicorn T-shirt said, snatching the dog from Olivia's hands before Olivia had a chance to respond.

Olivia's face contorted into what looked, to Skippy, like pre-explosion rage. He quickly but kindly took the dog from the girl's hands and handed it back to Olivia. He asked the little plush-animal-grabber to please inspect the flower he had pinned to his lapel and to let him know if it looked alright. After she confirmed that it looked fine, he made a show of inspecting it, squirting himself in the face with a stream of water from the flower just as he pretended to take an extra good look. That was enough to diffuse the situation.

He led them in a game of Simon Says, complete with prat falls and other silly acts of clumsiness and when they all seemed to be relaxed and having fun, he got out his walking stick and one-by-one asked each child to greet his friend, Mr. Frog, with an extra loud welcoming *ribbit*. He twirled the walking stick like a baton, tossed it in the air several times, then paraded them around the yard, using the walking stick like a drum major uses his mace, while playing "If You're Happy and You Know It" on the kazoo. He stopped to face the kids each time it came to the part in the song that called for an action, so he could show the kids—if they were happy and they knew it—what they were supposed to do.

Skippy and the parade of children arrived back at the slab of cement and finally it was time for balloon animals. Skippy could feel the sweat running down his back under his green silk shirt and over-sized plaid wool jacket. He grabbed his hand pump and shoved a handful of balloons into his jacket pocket. The walking sticks, he left leaning against his trunk of props.

He was busy making the third balloon wiener dog when two wasps came down and stung him on his neck. He batted wildly at them and noticed more swarming around from a nest they'd built on the underside of the porch eave that overhung the cement slab. In an instant he'd grabbed his walking stick and, in a single swing, brought the bulk of the nest to the ground where he stomped on it with his giant clown shoe in hopes of doing away with the stinging insects.

"He killed our pollinators!" Olivia sobbed inconsolably as if the fate of the planet rested with the wasps at her address.

"I think we've had enough," Olivia's mother said, directing him to gather his belongings while she darted into the house to grab his payment.

"Looks like someone rained on your parade," Roger Soukup said when Stanley arrived back at the motel.

Roger and his wife, Minerva, who worked together painting houses for a living, were sitting outside their room with the door ajar, as they often did on weekend afternoons, watching the traffic on the highway.

"It's been a pretty rough day."

Roger reached inside the door and pulled out an empty plastic storage crate for Stanley to sit on. Roger and Minerva had been staying in 123 for as long as Stanley had been in 125. About a third of the rooms were taken up by people who considered the Havana Inn their temporary home. Each room had a microwave, a coffee pot, and a mini refrigerator. Between them, there were an assortment of toasters, electric griddles, crockpots, and table-top charcoal grills. Occasionally they pooled their efforts and enjoyed a potluck, of sorts, in the stretch of sidewalk outside their rooms. It was nice to have neighbors to visit with.

"It was awful," Stanley said, filling Roger and Minerva in on the details of the party. "I like clowning, I mean I love clowning for the old folks. I just don't like working with kids, I guess. I mean, I like kids and all. Not that I've been around many, except in my clown work. It's just...I guess I don't relate to them, and some of them are downright obnoxious, and I wish it wasn't the paying part of my clowning, but I need the money."

"Ever thought about drag?" Roger asked.

"Huh?"

"Drag, you know dressing up like a woman. Pays better, you know. No kids to worry about. And that joint on the east edge of town, the place that used to be a buffet by the truck stop, they have a drag night about twice a month, I think. Usually on Saturdays."

Stanley thought for a while. "I guess a person can do it even if they aren't a drag queen," he said. "I mean Flip Wilson and Milton Berle dressed up like women for some of their comedy scenes, if I'm remembering right." How his mother had loved those old variety shows from her youth when they came back on cable.

"There you go," Roger said.

Stanley lay in bed that night, going over options. In a way, drag really was like clowning. He was an expert with heavy make-up applications, knew his way around wigs, and with clothes and shoes that weren't quite made to fit his body. And he wasn't opposed to sequins and sparkles. Though he wasn't great with people, being on stage didn't unnerve him, in fact he kind of liked it. And he knew about projecting a persona and engaging a crowd. Many of the basic skills, it seemed, he had covered. And best of all...no kids.

He woke Sunday morning, feeling unsettled. Lunch was nearly over when he parked at Happy Manor. Hopefully Connie and the gang were still at their table. Gordon's place was empty when he arrived in the dining room.

"He's been in the hospital for two days with pneumonia," Connie said. "Sounds like he's not doing well. His kids are on their way."

It felt like a punch in the gut. Still, he came to get the opinion of the people he felt closest to since his mom was gone, and both Connie and Gordon nearly treated him as if he was their own.

"I say go for it," Connie said. "What do you have to lose? You can always quit and find something else if you don't like it. But don't forget your friends at Happy Manor, we still need a little clown fun once in a while."

"Absolutely, I'd never quit on my friends here," he said. "You all are the best."

Just then Lana reached in to clear the table and just as quickly she was gone.

"There's where you really should be focusing your efforts," Connie said.

"What do you mean?" Stanley's stomach did a little flip flop at Connie's suggestion and a rush of warmth and excitement came over him.

"Lana, she likes you, you know."

"What do you mean she likes me? She doesn't say anything to me when I'm here and she didn't even look at me when she was here clearing the table."

"That's because she likes you, dummy," Connie said. "Trust me, you don't get to be my age without knowing a thing or two."

When the tables were cleared and the room was back in order, Stanley noticed Lana going for a break and he followed her outside. They sat at a picnic table while she drank her soda.

"Would you like to go out for coffee some time when you get off work?" he asked. "Maybe even today if you're not busy."

"I'd love that," she said. He hadn't noticed before how pretty she was when she smiled.

He asked her some things about her work at Happy Manor and she asked about his clowning. He told her about the birthday party and about his conversation with Roger.

"Would it bother you to go to coffee with a fellow who's thinking about dressing up like a drag queen?" he asked.

She took a sip of her soda and looked him straight in the eye. "Not in the least."

About the author:

Marilee Aufdenkamp is recently retired after nearly a quarter century teaching undergraduate nursing. She is currently at work on her second novel-length piece of historical fiction—the first remains unpublished. She has had half a dozen short stories published in electronic and small circulation print journals. She recently launched a Facebook group called Twentieth Century Historical Chat where members honor the quotidian lives of parents, grands, and greats, and celebrate their own childhoods and their twentieth century coming-of-age experiences. Marilee and her husband live in a smallish town in Nebraska and are the proud parents of a grown daughter whom they rely on heavily for tech support.

THE ROYAL BOIL
©2025 by Phillip Lynne

The castle stood on the hilltop, splendid in the sunshine and powerful in its solid rock walls. With spires displaying the banners of the royal family, it boasted a total of fifty-seven rooms, each functional in its appointed task and fully endowed with costly furnishings gathered from the far corners of the known world.

In one of these rooms, the topmost of the eastern tower, King Derrido stood before his full-length mirror and adjusted his royal attire. The silk and satin were of superior quality, and he liked the way it fit his muscular, albeit short body. His flowing red hair reached his collars and framed a face that was stern, rugged, and manly.

"You're such a handsome devil," he told his reflection. "I'd fall in love with you myself if I wasn't already myself and was someone else." He frowned at the strangeness of his own words. "Well, you know what I mean." The reflection smiled back.

King Derrido crossed the room to a dressing table and sat down, a gasp bursting from his lips as a terrible pain shot through his lower extremities. He jumped to his feet, supported himself on the table with his right hand, and rubbed his right buttock with his left hand. Not an easy thing to do, but King Derrido prided himself on his dexterity.

"Holy Forsooth!" he cried. "That really smarts!" He studied his chair to find the source of the pain, but the lush velvet seat was unmarred and smooth. The realization then hit him that the pain was not caused by a foreign object in his chair but existed as the result of a large protrusion on his right buttock cheek, which was sore to the touch.

Moving back across the room while pulling down his tights, the king backed up to the mirror. Staring over his shoulder, he beheld a purple raised area about an inch across. He touched it gingerly and was rewarded with another stabbing pain. He quickly pulled the servant call rope hanging next to the mirror.

Ten minutes later, the royal bedchamber door opened and a tall, lanky man with an enormous nose entered. "You called, Sire?"

"About time you showed your scurvy hide, Sniffington," the king growled. "What kept you?"

Sniffington looked down his nose. "I was involved in overseeing that most joyous of duties: the cleaning out of your kennels. Really, Sire, we need to check on the diet those dogs are receiving. Way too much fiber. Perhaps if we increased their intake of cheese, it would lessen..."

"Shut up, Sniffington! I've got more important things to think about. Just look at this." The king turned his back and dropped his tights again.

"Good Lord, what a boil!" Sniffington shouted before he could stop himself. He cleared his throat and regained his composure. "That must be quite painful, Sire."

"Hurts like a mother-humper," Derrido responded. "Get something and lance it. There are some hatpins over on the dressing table."

There was an explosion of air through the butler's lips as he tried to repress a laugh. "You can't be serious."

"Of course, I'm serious! There must be *fifty* hatpins over there."

"No, no, Sire. I mean you can't be serious about having *me* lance your boil."

"Why? Think you're too good?"

"Frankly, Sire—yeah. I mean that sort of thing was not included in my job description."

"Job description? I didn't know you had a job description."

"I assure you I do. A member of my family has been a manservant to your family for countless generations. A strict set of rules has been passed down from father to son detailing allowable duties. Believe me, Sire, lancing a boil on your royal bum is not included among them."

"Damn and blast!" the king snapped. "Right, call the Royal Butt Lancer, then!"

"I believe there is no such thing as the Royal Butt Lancer, Sire."

Derrido frowned. "You're joking. I've got a Royal Enema Giver, for God's sake! Not to mention a Royal Toe Jam Remover, a Royal Bellybutton Lint Puller, and a Royal Earwax Sucker. And you're telling me we have no Royal Butt Lancer?"

"I'm afraid not."

King Derrido pulled himself up to his full four-foot height. "We'll create a new position, then. I hereby order you to find me a Royal Butt Lancer before nightfall, Sniffington. I don't care who it is. Anybody at all. *Anybody* at all! Do you understand me?"

"Yes, Sire," Sniffington said, turning to leave.

"Well...it should be someone with soft hands, of course."

"Of course, Sire," the manservant replied, continuing toward the door.

"And a man, I suppose."

"Certainly, Sire."

"I mean we can't have a woman looking at the royal tush now, can we?"

"Heaven forbid, Sire."

"But a *manly* man, Sniffington."

"Obviously, Sire."

"Can't have a non-manly man looking at the royal tush either."

"Definitely not, Sire."

"You think I'm a moron, don't you, Sniffington?"

"Indubitably, Sire."

The door closed behind the manservant.

***

Peter Pitcher heaved on the pitchfork, sending a pile of horse "apples" flying out the stable door. There was a sudden string of curses from outside and Peter leaned his disheveled blonde head around the door.

"Oh, sorry about that, gov! Didn't see you standing there in the doorway."

"I wasn't *standing* in the doorway," Sniffington told him as he brushed his clothes off. "I was entering the stable to procure my steed."

"Eh? You were going to do *what* to your steed? I think that sort of thing is illegal, gov. I mean, far be it from me to question what a man does to his own 'orse, but there *are* the laws to consider. I mean, they create such laws to keep down the sort of decadence you're talking about. I mean, where would we be without laws like that? In turmoil, that's where. Pure turmoil. I can't stand turmoil. Never could. So, if you don't mind, gov, take your horse outside before you do whatever it is you said you was going to do to 'im. I mean, I do 'ave to keep up appearances and all, don't I?"

"I was going to *procure* my horse, you cretin."

"Right, and you still can. I won't stand in your way. Just take 'im outside before you get started. There's a good chap."

Sniffington suppressed his anger. "On second thought, I don't think I'll be needing my horse after all. What's your name, fool?"

The stableman squinted. "Peter, sir. But don't be getting any notions about procuring me. I'm a family man, I am. Got me a wife of the female persuasion and I'm quite happy with that arrangement, if you don't mind."

"Oh, do shut up, will you? I've got a new job for you, Peter."

"I don't know about that, Squire. I mean, I got me a fancy position in the stables 'ere and I don't know as I'm looking for a change. Sure, it don't pay but five quid a year, but I gets to keep warm and sling all the nasty stuff I can 'andle. Them 'orses can lay it down, believe you me, gov. Never-ending supply of the stuff, actually. I think if I could ever figure out a way to turn it into food, I would make a fortune and run the king out..."

"I'll have your tongue cut out if you don't *shut your hole!*" Sniffington shouted.

"Careful, friend," Peter Pitcher told him. "Turning that shade of green can't be good for the body, or the soul."

Sniffington reached out, caught the stableman by his left ear, and dragged him from the stables.

King Derrido looked up as the door opened. He sized up the man who entered, taking in the dirty shoes, the dirty pants, the dirty shirt, the dirty face, and the dirty hair. He gagged when the dirty smell hit him.

"Who are you?"

"Peter Pitcher's the name, Your Majesty."

"You're an absolute mess!"

"Well, now, I would be, wouldn't I? Seeing as I'm the stableman. Being without benefit of fancy clothes and access to a bath at least once a month and all, like some. Your royal self included."

"What's the meaning of this, Sniffington?"

The manservant beamed and held out his hands as if offering the king a tray of delicious morsels. "The Royal Butt Lancer, Your Highness."

"The *what*?" Peter Pitcher asked.

The bathhouse air smelled of lilac-scented perfume. Peter Pitcher, however, was not inhaling at the moment. He was under the warm water in a gold-covered bathtub. As he surfaced, he spit a stream of water in a fair imitation of a fountain.

"So, what's all this about a butt lancer?" he asked Sniffington, who was holding a towel by the door.

"I would prefer that the King discuss that matter with you."

"Well, it sounds a trifle strange to me," the now clean stableman said. "You know what I told you about being a family man and all at the stable."

"I don't think you have to worry about that," Sniffington replied. "It's not that sort of thing."

The door behind him opened and King Derrido entered. He smiled when he saw Peter. "All cleaned up and presentable, are we?"

"I believe so, Your Grace," Peter said. "Your lackey 'ere 'as made sure of everything. Even looked in me ears to make I sure I didn't just 'it the 'igh spots."

The king looked pleased. "Excellent, then. Now, Peter Pitcher, I'd like your judgment on something."

"Lay it out, Your Eminence. I'm sure I'll come up with an opinion on whatever it is."

"I have no doubt on that point either," Sniffington said under his breath.

King Derrido turned, pulled down his tights, and pushed his rear end toward the new Royal Butt Lancer. "What do you think of this?"

Peter closed one eye and turned his head to one side, paused, then reversed eyes and head position. "Well, blimey, Sire, I don't know. It's nice and all that, but I'd say a couple weeks shoveling horse muck would firm that bum right up and make all the ladies start looking at you like you was a new man. Might even get yourself a..."

"Not the *shape* of his derriere, you ass!" Sniffington huffed. "He's asking what you think of the boil."

Peter opened both eyes and leaned forward. "Bloody 'ell! 'Ow could I 'ave missed that? Why, I could drive a carriage-and-six through that thing, if it 'ad an opening! I'd 'ave that seen to, if I were you."

King Derrido turned to face him. "Right, that's your mission. How do you propose to handle it?"

"You want *me* to take care of the boil?"

"That's your job now," Snuffington informed him.

Understanding flashed in Peter's eyes. "Oh, right, I get it! Cor, sometimes I suppose a brick 'ouse *does* have to fall on me in order for me to see the light! The Royal Butt Lancer, that's me now. Well, bugger! And 'ere I thought you gentlemen was trying to turn me 'ead from the ladies. I must say, that's a load off me mind. I was beginning to think I'd 'ave to thrash you both soundly in order to get away. Don't like physical violence, mind you, but..."

"So?" the king urged. "How would you handle this situation?"

Peter rubbed his chin. "Well, that's the thing now, isn't it? 'Ow to take care of a boil the size of a Yorkshire Pudding."

"Oh, come off it," Derrido said. "It's not *that* bloody big."

"You should come round 'ere where I'm sitting, Your Lordship. It's big enough to load into one of them cannons outside, if you ask me."

"He was thinking of using a hatpin," Sniffington offered.

Peter nodded thoughtfully while reaching out and poking the boil gently with his finger. "A 'atpin might do the task, it being sharp and all. We'd 'ave to make sure it was absolutely clean before we go ramming it into the thing. Wouldn't want his kingship picking up some type of virus, or even a fungus at the very worst. I 'ad a stable boy what was apprenticing under me about a year ago. Cut 'imself on a nail in the stable. Laid 'is bleeding arm open from elbow to wrist. In just two days, 'is wound got infected and swelled up enormous, just like your boil there, Your Honor. Of course, 'e more than likely got a bit of horse muck in it, which I'm sure 'elped the infestation along. We tried everything with that lad, but nothing worked. Finally, the doctor 'ad to amputate his arm just above the elbow. I don't even think the worms would feast on that severed limb, it was that nasty..."

"If I have to tell you to shut up one more time," the King said between clenched teeth, "you'll swing from the highest rampart in the castle."

"Well now, that sounds like quite a bit of fun and..."

"By your neck."

"Oh. Fetch the 'atpin!"

Peter Pitcher held the hatpin up to the window and squinted at it. "Looks to be sharp enough. Should do the job quite nicely."

King Derrido was on his stomach across a barrel, which Sniffington had rolled into the bathhouse. "Is it going to hurt?"

Peter smiled. "I don't rightly see 'ow it wouldn't, Your

Magnificence. We *are* talking about 'alf a meter of cold steel being shoved into your royal sit-down."

The King's eyes grew wide. "Half a meter? Surely you're not going to use the entire hatpin!"

"If that thing keeps growing like it is, I may 'ave to run fetch me pitchfork and use *that*. Right, Sniffles, your turn. Swab his bum down with that whiskey I asked for."

"It's *Sniffington*," the manservant said. "And swab his bum down yourself." He held out the bottle.

"I'm the Royal Butt *Lancer*," Peter told him. "I'll 'ave to ask for more pay if I 'ave to be the Royal Butt *Swabber*, too."

Derrido shouted, "You are both going to be Royal Sewer Workers if you don't get on with it!"

Peter mumbled something below his breath and quickly splashed whiskey across the king's rump. "Right, that does it for the antiseptic. Brace yourself, Your Glory, 'ere comes the 'atpin!"

Derrido steeled himself, eyes closed, teeth clenched. When nothing happened for thirty seconds, he looked up. "What are you doing?"

"Trying to decide the best way to do this," Peter said. "I mean, I could come at you straight on but can't guarantee I could stop the 'atpin before it 'its one of your vital organs. On the other 'and, if I go at it from the side, the pin would slide nicely through without a worry as to what it was 'itting on the other side."

Sniffington sighed. "Then the second option sounds the most preferable. Get on with it, man."

Peter glanced at the butler. "And what if I *do* go in from the side and I push too 'ard and the 'atpin keeps going? I picture an enormous rip in the royal butt that will take a long time to 'eal. Are you going to follow 'is Brilliance around with a cushion the entire time 'e's curing to make sure 'e sits comfortable?"

"Not I," Sniffington said.

"Well then, I'd better sit and think on this some more."

"Good Lord, we'll be here all day if we wait for you to come up with *another* thought. I'm sure you reached your monthly quota with the first."

"What does that mean?" Peter asked, moving to stand in front of the manservant.

"Figure it out yourself, muck jockey."

"I've 'ad just enough of that snooty air you've got, Sniffles."

"I'd think it would be a refreshing air after what you're used to in that stable where you live."

"And I would think that you'll get a lot of relief after I let out some of that 'ot air that's got you swelled up like a dead pig in the 'ot sun!" Peter raised the hatpin.

"*That's enough!*" King Derrido screamed and tried to get to his feet. The barrel shifted suddenly, and he spun almost fully around. Trying to regain his balance, he tripped over his tights and fell backward, his buttocks slapping hard on the stone floor.

"Your Majesty!" Sniffington cried and reached out to help the king to his feet.

Derrido allowed himself to be pulled up. A frown was on his face as he reached around with his right hand. Then a smile spread from ear to ear. "It's gone!"

Peter asked, "What's gone?"

"The boil, you buffoon! The fall must have popped it! See? It's not there anymore!"

Peter winced. "Ewww, that's awfully disgusting. Sniffles, what color would you say that stuff oozing out is?"

"*Get him out of here!*" King Derrido commanded.

Peter Pitcher hefted another full pitchfork and tossed it out the door. Richard Lob, Peter's new apprentice, sat on the windowsill and watched him.

"This stinks, Peter. I need to look for another line of work."

"Don't go talking like that, Dicky. You got it made 'ere! Believe me, I've been out in the real world and I learnt a thing or two."

"Yeah? Like what?"

"Like this stable 'ere is the only 'eaven I'll ever need." He turned to look at his apprentice and smiled. "And that everything else out there is nothing but a royal pain in the arse."

About the author:

Phillip Lynne lives in Tennessee and unleashes stories on an unsuspecting world. He has been published in five countries—most of them on Earth.

A CLASH OF DREAMS
©2025 by Evan Slebowitz

Isaac came awake suddenly, clutching at his chest, a scream on his lips. The dream had come again. At first, he had no idea where he was, panic from the dream a living thing inside him. Dark as pitch, there was nothing for his eyes to focus on. The smell of leather and sweat permeated the hot, stifling air, and the sound of snoring caused him to remember the tent he shared with five other men.

Isaac turned onto his back, his lungs gasping for any semblance of fresh air. The tent fabric sagged and brushed his face. A wave of claustrophobia mixing with the panic of the dream, made it necessary to leave the smothering tent. He clawed his way over the man next to him, provoking shouted curses as he threw open the tent flap and half-ran, half-fell into the night.

He dropped to his knees and gulped the cool air, the dream fading with every breath. An easy breeze, blowing from the east, brought much needed relief to his sweat-soaked body. After two minutes, he stood and looked around. The hillside where he was standing was a virtual sea of white tents, each swelling and shrinking with the breeze. A half-moon hung on the clear horizon, casting long, deep shadows. Somewhere, the cry of a Whippoorwill echoed.

For the first time in many days, the world was quiet for nineteen-year-old Isaac Overholt, foot soldier in the Army of the Potomac. The war seemed a million miles away from this part of northern

Virginia and peace reigned on his little hillside.

"Can't sleep, Isaac?"

Startled, he whirled to find the silhouette of a tall man. "Good Lord, Robert, you've scared the life out of me!"

Robert Wallace was Isaac's senior by ten years. "I was on my way back from the hole when I saw you over here. Anything wrong?"

"I just had a bad dream. It's got me worried, Robert."

"Tell me about it."

Isaac hesitated, afraid that talking about the dream, transferring somewhat out-of-focus images to actual words, might somehow make it come true. "I...it's come every night now for the last five nights and it's the same each time."

Robert sat on the ground, stretched out his long legs, and leaned back on his hands. He waited for Isaac to sit also. "Let's hear it."

The younger soldier inhaled. "All right. At first, I'm standing in a forest somewhere. Nobody is in sight, but I know there's a battle going on because I can hear cannon and men shouting. And there's smoke everywhere. Real thick and hanging low, you know what I mean? My rifle's empty and I'm trying desperately to reload it, but my fingers feel as thick as fence posts. I keep dropping everything. Then some Rebs come out of the smoke, screaming like demons from hell. I start retreating..."

"Withdrawing," Robert corrected, a finger raised. "You are withdrawing in an orderly fashion. Don't you ever listen to what your officers tell you?"

Isaac laughed. "All right, I start withdrawing in an orderly fashion, but I'm still dropping things. I tell you, Robert, I'm scared to death at this point in the dream. There's a rifle shot close to me and I'm away, running like a scalded hare, just waiting for a bullet in the back. Somehow, I get my rifle reloaded, spin around, and come face to face with a Reb. He's about my age and we just stand there staring at each other for the longest time. That's all, just staring. Then he starts laughing. And it's a terrible laugh, Robert, like coming from the devil himself. It gets louder and louder until I can't hear the fight going on around us."

"He sounds like a happy sort," Robert says with a smile. "Then what?"

"He shoots me," Isaac said, burying his face in his hands. "My dear Lord, he shoots me in the chest. I can feel the bullet plow into my chest and my eyes start to die, everything going black. Then I wake up."

"That's some nightmare."

"What do you think it means?"

Robert shook his head. "That's not for me to say. I don't play around with that kind of thing. If I don't understand it, it's not meant for me to."

Isaac stared at the ground. "I think it means I'm to die in the next battle."

"Nonsense. Not possible. We've been in over ten battles together. Look at us, Isaac. Not a scratch. And we're always in the thick of things, too, not hiding in the rear with the wounded like some do."

"My Granny told us she dreamed of her death and she *did*, two days later."

"Of what, old age? Come on, Isaac, get it out of your head. Think about something else."

"I've tried, but the dream is so real. I'm truly scared, Robert. Do you think there will be a battle in the morning?"

Robert chuckled. "I saw some officers packing their kits and heading for the rear. If that's not a sure sign there's a fight coming up, I don't know what is. Don't worry! You'll be singing songs around the fire tonight just like always."

"Listen, I've written a letter, and I want your promise that you'll take it to my family after I fall."

"I want no more talk like that, do you hear?" Robert's voice dropped low, but he took the letter nonetheless. "Talk like that could jinx all of us. Look, somebody watches out for people like you and me. How else do you think we've survived this long? We've got protection, a *divine shield* around us. I think that's how the preacher put it. We live good, don't cause any trouble, and we're fighting on God's side. I tell you, Isaac, there's not a Reb bullet made that can hit us while we're protected like we are. So, for heaven's sake, cheer up would you?"

Isaac got to his feet. "I hope you're right, Robert. I hope to God you're right."

Joshua Trendle sat bolt upright, shocked awake by a dream. He stood and leaned against the tree covering his bed of pine needles. Shaking all over, he was more scared than he had ever been in his fifteen-year-old life. He closed his eyes and saw scraps of the fading dream, the Yankee soldier firing, the ball tearing through his skull, the world going dark....

A hint of gray on the horizon told him it was almost morning. There was to be a battle today, the officers said so. The word going around was that the Yankees were nearby and spoiling for a fight. "Revenge for all the whuppings we been giving 'em," his sergeant had said. "They'll be hell-bent to pay us back."

Joshua felt cold fingers of fear creep up his spine. He was going to die in this battle. Sure as the sun was coming up, he was going to die today. The dream was too real for it to be otherwise.

He knelt and felt around in his backpack, pulling out a small Bible his mother had given him. He couldn't read, but he got a great deal of comfort from just holding it against his chest.

"Keep this with you at all times, Joshua," Momma had said at the train station, pressing it into his hands. "That way God will always be by your side and protect you. He believes in what we're fighting for, and He'll see that we win and send those Bluebellies back North where they belong."

As he clutched the Bible, he realized that today was his mother's birthday. Surely, he wouldn't be killed on Momma's birthday! She could never enjoy her birthday knowing that her only son had been killed on her special day. God would never let that happen. She was too good a person to have her birthday ruined like that.

There was movement to his left and he saw the company bugler making his way quietly over and around the sleeping soldiers. The bugler was going to signal the start of the day, calling the Southern army to rise and march off to battle with flags flying and drums pounding.

And he would die.

The sudden urge to stop the bugler, to take the instrument away from him and fling it into the nearby river, came over Joshua. Without the bugle, the army couldn't wake up. They would miss the battle and he would live!

"It won't work," Joshua told himself, fighting back tears. There's no stopping it. The battle will come. The war would go on. The world would continue its gallop toward total destruction. He looked over at the church tent and wondered if the army chaplain was awake. Perhaps if he could talk to him and tell him how scared he was of the dream, of the battle, of dying....

The clear, bold call of the bugle echoed across the field.

A rider approached Company H at full gallop. "Captain Rogers!" he shouted, reining his horse and saluting. "Colonel Pinchon requests that you move your company over that hill in support of the artillery. The Rebels are pushing in this direction and are expected to break through shortly. Companies F on your right and D on your left will move with you."

Captain Rogers returned the salute. "All right, Corporal. Inform Colonel Pinchon we shall move out immediately." He turned and repeated the orders to his men.

Isaac Overholt stood with the others, shouldered his Springfield rifle, and took his place in the front rank. "Looks as if our turn has come."

Robert Wallace, on his right, adjusted his cap. "High time! Can't stand the waiting."

The battle had been joined shortly after daybreak. Company H, initially held in reserve, moved forward in stages as the other reserve units were drawn into the fray. Having occupied their current position for two hours, the men had made themselves comfortable in the tall grass.

"I'll take the waiting," Isaac said, eyeing the hill to the front of the company. Some distance beyond, columns of black smoke rose into the sky, the stutter of rifle fire increasing in volume.

Captain Rogers glanced to his left and right while pulling his sword. "Company H! At the quick step! Forward!"

The men stepped off as one and moved up the hill at a jog, the companies to either side doing the same. Three artillery batteries occupied positions on the summit to the left and maintained a steady rate of fire, shrouded in their own smoke.

"You have my letter, don't you?" Isaac asked Robert.

"Of course I do. The best thing for you to do is forget that nonsense and see to the task at hand."

"How can I forget it?"

"Well, just try taking a look at *that*."

The battlefield unfolded as they crested the hill and started down the other side, a four hundred-yard slope into thick forest. A line of Federal troops, deployed just short of the trees, was firing into the woods and receiving heavy fire in return, the number of casualties increasing with each second.

A chill passed through Isaac. "Oh, Lord," he said under his breath, "keep us from those trees." He glanced at Robert, who could read a battlefield as one would read a roadmap.

"Those boys aren't going to hold," the older man said. "See how the line is bending in the middle? The Rebs will charge when it breaks, and then we'll be in the thick of it."

"Let them come. As long as we stay clear of the trees, I'll not argue."

"Speak for yourself. As for me, I would *prefer* the trees. Beats standing out here in the open."

"But my dream is in those trees," Isaac whispered.

When the company was one hundred yards down the hill, Captain Rogers shouted, "All right, men, we'll form our line here." He held out his right arm as a reference point.

At that moment, the artillery batteries opened fire with a thunderous volley, solid shot passing overhead with a crack and whistle that set Isaac's teeth on edge. Seconds later, the edge of the forest shuddered under the weight of the projectiles.

"That cleaned 'em out!" a man behind Isaac shouted. "Not many Rebs left after that, I'd wager!"

Robert leaned close to Isaac's ear. "See to your weapon, Isaac. They'll be coming soon. Those shots were much too low."

Captain Rogers was of the same opinion. "Fix bayonets. Get ready for their charge."

Isaac pulled his bayonet from its scabbard and fixed it to his rifle. He then hoisted the weapon and pulled the hammer back to the half-cock position. Having gone through the process of loading the weapon earlier, he finished the task by taking a percussion cap from a pouch on his belt and placing it on the rifle's cone.

"Our boys are taking an awful pounding," Robert was saying. "They're about ready to break and run."

The Federal line was beginning to sag away from the trees as those in the middle withdrew. Again, the cannons thundered, shattering the forest's edge. Isaac remembered the Whippoorwill's call and longed for the quiet of last night.

Captain Rogers strode back and forth. "They'll be coming soon. Check your rifles. Make sure they're loaded up proper. We'll pour a volley into 'em soon as they're in range. After that, reload and we'll hit 'em again. By then, the cannon boys will be ready with canister and grapeshot." He stopped suddenly and turned.

The Union line had broken, the soldiers taking to their heels. Confederate troops emerged from the trees with a terrible shout and quickly dressed themselves into a long line three ranks deep and began moving up the hill.

Rogers drew his sword. "Here they come, boys!"

As the routed soldiers came within earshot, Rogers waved his sword. "Fall in with us, men! Turn your guns to 'em and give 'em hell!"

While some stopped and took places at the ends of the company, most didn't look back as they ran up and over the hill.

Isaac fingered the trigger guard of his rifle. The Confederates had slowed their advance to a quick walk, rifles at the ready. The Union cannons opened fire again, this time with explosive shells, their burning fuses visible as they arced across the field. Detonating both in the air and on the ground, the shells tore gaping holes in the Confederate lines, which were quickly filled by men from the rear ranks.

While staring at the advancing gray line, Isaac kept his gaze low, focusing on belt buckles and canteens, anything but the enemy's eyes. Looking into their eyes made them human. He wondered which belt buckle was slated to kill him today.

Rogers turned his back to the Rebels. "All right, boys, volley fire at my command. Ready! "Remember, you are firing downhill, so shoot low. Aim!"

Rifles snapped to shoulders, the rear rank lowering their rifle barrels between the heads of the men in the front. Isaac steeled himself for the blast of the weapons that were inches from his ears. He sighted down his own rifle, locking it on a belt buckle.

Rogers dropped to his knees. "Fire!"

In an instant, Isaac's hearing was gone as over three hundred rifles fired simultaneously. The Confederate line disappeared behind a cloud of blue smoke. Isaac lowered the butt of his rifle to the ground and began the methodical process of reloading. His hands were shaking, his nostrils assaulted by the acrid smell of burnt gunpowder. He strained for a glimpse of the Confederate line to judge the effectiveness of the volley. A Stars and Bars flag appeared from the smoke, swaying somewhat, but still moving forward.

Rogers had his sword on high again, shouting for his men to prepare for the next volley. The third man on Isaac's left lurched forward, dropping his rifle and clutching his face. He fell to his knees before toppling over. Several more men dropped to the ground. Some fell slowly, struggling to maintain their balance, others fell like trees under an ax.

Robert came close to Isaac's ear and shouted, "This volley will be the last. They're trying to flank us on the right!"

Isaac looked at him and nodded. Several men beyond Robert

were on the ground. Further on, only the left end of Company F was visible in the smoke. Isaac was aware of his hearing beginning to return, his ears ringing, when a large group of gray-clad horsemen materialized on the right flank of Company F. With pistols and swords drawn, the Confederate cavalry crashed into the Federal line, breaking it, the men turning to run without discharging their weapons.

"Fire!" Rogers screamed, unaware of the chaos on his right.

The second volley came apart, some soldiers firing forward, others turning to meet the cavalry charge, Isaac included. Several horses went down with terrible screams, yet the momentum of the charge was not impeded. Isaac began reloading, but Robert was pushing hard on his shoulder.

"No time, Isaac!" he shouted. "Run!"

Isaac spun on his heel into mass confusion. Panic was spreading across the Federal line in a wave. The Confederate cavalry had worked their way behind them, pushing the surprised soldiers back into the face of the advancing infantry. Isaac stumbled and went down as a soldier with a wound to the gut fell against him.

Robert appeared and pulled him to his feet. "Get out of here!" he shouted and pointed. "That way, behind you!"

Isaac turned again but saw no place to go. The Rebel infantry was on them now, the fighting hand-to-hand, bayonets slashing. He felt Robert's hand in his back, then he was stumbling forward, his own bayonet held high. Suddenly, the way was open in front of him. He brought his rifle close across his chest and ran through the opening.

Straight toward the trees.

Joshua Trendle observed the fighting on the hill from deep within the forest. His company was being held back to ensure the woods remained in Confederate hands, which suited him just fine. Though the hill was covered in smoke, he could see that the Federals were in no shape to attempt a counterattack.

"We're winnin' out on this'un," he said to no one in particular.

"Yep," the man next to him replied. "Them bluebellies is done sent for. They'll be hidin' under their mommas' skirts fore nightfall."

Joshua grinned and settled himself on his bedroll. While most of the battle had been close enough to observe, he had not yet fired his rifle. He rubbed the Bible in his left hand and glanced upward through the trees. The dream wasn't going to come true after all! The Lord was watching out for him, keeping him away from danger. At least for today. And today was all he could ask for.

"Here now, little pup," the man next to him muttered. "Where you think you're off to?"

Joshua followed his gaze. A Yankee soldier had emerged from the smoke on the hill, and was coming straight on for the trees, reloading his rifle as he ran.

"He's goin' in the wrong direction," Joshua said. "What's he doin'?"

"Addled in the head, most likely, and shittin' himself with every step."

The captain of Joshua's company got to his feet. "Trendle, make that Yank a prisoner."

Almost as if he had heard, the Union soldier abruptly changed direction. Still running hard, but on a new course parallel to the edge of the woods. Joshua hefted his rifle and moved off from his company to the left, dashing through the underbrush, trying to match the pace set by the Yankee.

A shout went up from the company as a Confederate horseman charged out of the smoke, saber flashing in the sun, riding hard in pursuit of the fleeing bluecoat.

Joshua noticed that the Yankee soldier, in turning from the threat of the cavalryman, had again changed direction. It was a close race, but it looked like he would make it to the trees before the horseman caught him.

Joshua increased his own pace, pushing through the underbrush with renewed vigor, the cheers and shouts of those in his company fading behind him. It was quieter in this part of the forest, some birds even managing to sing. He could hear the heavy breathing of the enemy soldier as he entered the trees, the pounding of the horse's hoofs, and the horseman's cry of triumph as he closed on his quarry.

Isaac Overholt was living his nightmare. He had fallen upon entering the shade of the forest, tripping over a hidden rock. He rolled over onto his back, pulling his rifle with him. The barrel snagged on a bush and he tugged furiously to free it. The Rebel cavalryman reigned his horse hard and leapt from the saddle, pulling his pistol.

"You run like a deer in them open fields," he said, cocking the weapon and pointing it at Isaac's head, "but in the trees you run like an old woman." He smiled, exposing dark stained teeth. "No room in this war for old women."

"Please," Isaac panted, his hands reaching out. He was overcome with fear, his voice high, coming in gasps. "Don't kill me."

The Rebel cackled, drowning out all other sounds. "But I *have* to kill you. You're the enemy."

Isaac was crying now, tears clouding his vision. The dream was real, it had come after all. Somewhere in the back of his brain, a prayer started. His blurred eyes locked on the man's trigger finger tightening, tightening.

The pistol went off and, for a split second, Isaac died, his heart stopping with the enormity of his fear. Then he was aware of dirt exploding next to his head and a weight falling onto his legs. He opened his eyes to find the cavalryman face down across his lower body. Another Rebel soldier, much younger than the first, stood looking down at him, his rifle held like a club.

"Nobody should enjoy killin' that much," Joshua Trendle said, rolling the man off the Yankee with his foot. "Up you come."

Isaac shook from head to toe as he took Joshua's hand. "Thank you."

Joshua shrugged. "Been enough killin' for the day." He looked around. "If'n you head that way and skirt the field, keepin' to the trees, you might jes' make it back to your friends."

Isaac squinted at him. "I can go?"

Joshua shrugged again. "I was supposed to take you prisoner, but like I say, too much killin' today. 'Sides, what would I do with you? I ain't got much food and I sure ain't wantin' to share it with no Yank." He smiled. "I'll have a bit of explainin' to do, but I'll think up somethin'."

Isaac moved away, not believing his luck. "Thanks. I appreciate this."

"Appreciate life," Joshua said. "There ain't enough of it."

Isaac held up his hand. "See ya in hell, Johnny Reb." He turned and began running, new energy flowing through his tired body.

Joshua returned the wave. "Yeah, but not today," he said, under his breath. "Only good dreams tonight."

About the author:

Stories are to Evan Slebowitz as slop is to hogs. He can't get enough. He lives to transfer tales from his brains to his computer, and then to the rest of humanity. He only hopes there is a receptive audience who appreciates his work.